Praise for Te

Tokens of Promise

Author Teresa Pollard puts this ......, steeped in ancient laws and customs, to the page in language I could easily understand and enjoy. Author's notes and a chapter by chapter Group Discussion Guide makes this book an educational and insightful tool for group as well as individual pleasure. Solid research coupled with author's well written imagination transforms the bare facts of their story into a tale of romance, intrigue, and God's plan to involve them in the direct genealogical line of Jesus Christ. A Wonderful Read! – Edna W.

Not Guilty (Windspree Book 1)

This is one of the best books that I have read lately. I loved how the authors put together a well written book. Rape is never pretty. As the story continues we see God's mighty hand at work in this situation. We find out that it is possible to take something so totally wrong and horrible and work a miracle out of it. – Judy B.

Not Ashamed (Windspree Book 2)

I could not put this book down! It was well written, tight, had no fluff that slowed the story down (and made one want to scream "get on with it!"), and it also was an honest rendering of several difficult subjects. This is how a book is supposed to be written! – Diginee

Woman of Light

A novel based on the life of Deborah

By Teresa Pollard

Dedicated to Krystal and Candi:
Two true women of light

Author's Note

The idea for this novel was born when my friend, Candi Pullen, told me that God had told her she was a "Deborah, sitting between the palm trees." She said she didn't have any idea what that meant. All she knew was that Deborah was the "wife of Lappidoth," and that she judged Israel for forty years.

Because of my study of Tamar, I was immediately able to tell her that the palm trees were symbolic of places of great sexual immorality because they were the *Asherah* groves where the women danced in their "religious" rites and practices. But her question intrigued me so I set about to research the subject more.

The first thing I found was that *Lappidoth* was a feminine plural form of the word, and therefore probably not a man's name at all. The word literally means torches or oil lamps. In fact, according to the Talmud, Barak the General was the husband of Deborah. This made perfect sense to me because I knew no self-respecting Jewish man would ever let his wife go off to war with another man for months at a time. Besides, why else would a General of the Israel's whole army listen to a woman in the first place? But I immediately knew this was going to put me in trouble with those Christians who tend to think I "stray" from the Bible. A better translation of *"eschet lapidot"* might be woman of light(s) or woman of splendor. Some scholars also suggest that it could be a city that was the place of Deborah's birth, although no such city has ever been found.

Some scholars also agree that Jacob's prophecy to Naphtali in Genesis 49:21 was a reference to Deborah. They also give this as further evidence that Barak was her husband since he was of the tribe of Naphtali.

The Talmud explains that selling torches or oil lamps was probably Barak's profession before he became Israel's General. They say, because of Deborah's cleverness at wick making, he became a wealthy man by selling wicks to the tabernacle at Shiloh and around the country. Again, this seemed perfectly logical to me.

I did some research on Jewish customs, traditions, and blessings to write this novel because I wanted it to be as authentic as possible, but unfortunately I have no practical experience in this area whatsoever, and I'm not sure that modern Jewish customs would reflect ancient ones much more than our Christian customs do. I only attended one synagogue service with my Hebrew professor back when I was at Hollins College. The only thing I distinctly remember about that experience was that my professor turned the lights on and off and switched on the coffee pot for them. So I apologize for any inaccuracies in this presentation.

Of course, the other "uh oh" was the story of Jael. It fascinates me that Jewish scholars have never had any problem discussing the sexual implications of a story. We really are "Puritans" in that we simply ignore them. There are two schools of Rabbinic thought. The first says that Sisera raped Jael seven times, and she killed him in the exact spot where he had raped her. They get this from the song of Deborah and Barak. I won't go into detail about that.

The second, and more modern, school says that Jael was divinely protected by *Adonai* from Sisera's lustful advances; that he supernaturally fell into a deep sleep when she hid him. Both admit she seduced him into coming into the tent with the intention of a sexual encounter, but that her actions were forgiven because they were taken as a brave sacrifice on Israel's behalf. Some scholars do believe she had her husband Heber's permission to sleep with Sisera, but whether that was for Israel's sake or to curry favor with Sisera is debatable. The Kenites were known for their great hospitality, and were pacifists in their beliefs. Harming someone to whom you had offered hospitality was definitely a cultural taboo.

I do admit that this novel is just that; a novel. There were twenty years for which I had absolutely no biblical evidence. This gap is represented by the break between "Book 1" and "Book 2" in the novel. In my Tamar story ("Tokens of Promise"), I had the entire book of Genesis to work out a family dynamics profile, but here I had almost nothing. I don't even know that Deborah was a granddaughter to Ehud. That was merely a supposition based on the thought that she had to have been taught the law somewhere, and what could be a more likely place than as a beloved grandchild of a lonely old man. It was most unusual idea to start with for a girl to be taught anything other than cooking or cleaning.

I tried to use the Song of Deborah and Barak as clues as to what might have happened during the 20 year gap in the story. Psychology 101 told me that there had to be an initial event that propelled two ordinary people into the events that changed their world. Since God had told Candi she was a "Deborah," I knew the one event Candi and I both had in common was losing a daughter. If Deborah had "beautiful fawns" and had somehow lost one of those daughters at the hands of Sisera, that would definitely be an impetus to action. Nevertheless, I freely admit this is simply speculation on my part, with no biblical evidence to support it.

For this story, I used the language of the Bible wherever it was given. Otherwise, I simply used modern English or the Hebrew, especially for words like mommy and daddy or grandma and granddaddy. I thought these might give the story a flavor of authenticity and help to transport the reader to another time and culture.

As usual, time and measurements were an obstacle to be kept to the forefront of this feeble imagination. There were no seconds or minutes or hours to be reckoned. All time was measured by the visible movement of the sun; i.e., something happened at "the breeze before the setting sun." The same is true for measurements — no feet or miles — only a "span" or a "cubit" or a day's journey.

I chose *Adonai* as the name for God I would use simply because I thought it would be the one Deborah would most likely use. The law had already been given. Jewish people did not speak the great name.

I suppose the thing that struck me the most about this story was something I'd never really thought about before yet I'd been doing all my life — the power of song, of praise to God. Moses and Miriam sang. Barak and Deborah sang. I love to sing. I don't do it nearly enough nowadays. Songs of praise please our heavenly Father greatly. Hebrews 13:15 tells us to "continually offer up a sacrifice of praise to God, that is, the fruit of lips that give thanks to His name."

When my godmother and my grandmother died three weeks apart, I often found myself singing the Gaithers' song, "Because He Lives." It soothed my soul in ways that are unexplainable, humanly speaking. When my daughter died, I again experienced that same reaction to song. It's almost impossible to truly sing praise to God and at the same time harbor bitterness or anger. The healing power of song on the human soul is truly one of our divine gifts. As we praise Him with our lips, He blesses us with healing for our hurting soul.

May God richly bless you as you continue to praise His name in song.

God bless,

Teresa Pollard

Glossary

Abba = Daddy

Abib = first month of Hebrew Calendar (now called Nisan)

Adonai = one of the Names of God

Asherah = plural form of *Ashtoreth,* used for worship of many goddesses

Ashtoreth = Canaanite fertility goddess (more commonly known as Astarte)

Baal/Baalim = male fertility god(s)

Bar mitzvah = the religious initiation ceremony of a Jewish boy who has reached the age of 13 and is regarded as ready to observe religious precepts and eligible to take part in public worship

Brit milah = circumcision ceremony

Brit milah blessing = *Baruch atah Adonai Eloheinu Melech ha-olam, asher kidshanu b'mitzvotav v'tzivanu l'hakhniso bivrito shel Avraham avinu.* (Blessed are You, *Adonai* our God, King of the Universe, who has sanctified us with Your commandments and commanded us to bring him [the child] into the covenant of Abraham, our Father.)

Chalaka = first haircut celebration

Chesed = loving-kindness

Cubit = measurement from the tip of an adult male's middle finger to his elbow (approximately 18 inches)

Deborah = little bee

Dohd = uncle

Eschet lapidot = woman of light

Halal = praise

Hametz = leaven (symbolic of sin)

HaSatan = Satan

Ima = Mommy

Kippah = Skullcap

Kwater = Godfather/guardian

Mensch = a person of integrity and honor

Mitzvah = good deed done because of religious duty

Mohar = bridal dowry

Mohel = circumciser

Molech = Canaanite god

Omer = fluid measurement: 1/10 of an Ephah (approximately 3 and 2/3 liters)

Pesach = Passover

Saba = Grandfather

Safta = Grandmother

Shabbat = *Sabbath*

Shabbat blessing = *Baruch atah Adonai Eloheinu Melech ha-olam, asher kidshanu m'mitzvotav v'tzivanu l'hadlik ner shel Shabbat.* (Blessed are You, *Adonai* our God, King of the Universe, Who made us wholly by Your precepts, and commanded us to light the *Sabbath* lights.)

Shachar = dawn

Shalom = a greeting of peace

Shekel = a basic monetary unit

Sheol = the abode of the dead

Shavuot = Festival of First Fruits

Span = measurement from a man's thumb to his pinkie with hand outspread (approximately 6 inches)

Sukkoth = Festival of Booths

Tallith = prayer shawl

Zayith = olive

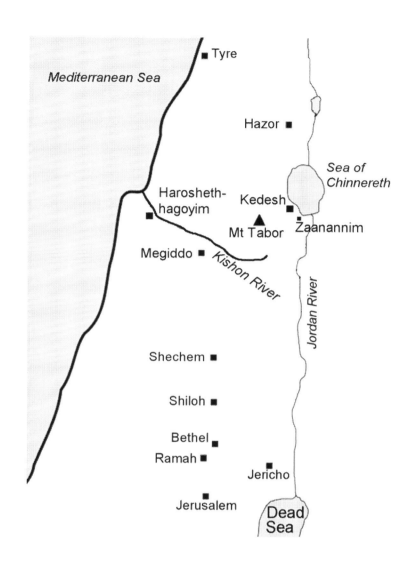

BOOK ONE

The Lord is my light and my salvation;
Whom shall I fear? The Lord is the defense of my life; whom shall I dread?
Psalm 27:1

CHAPTER
1

So Moab was subdued that day under the hand of Israel. And the land was undisturbed for eighty years. Judges 3:30

Deborah tried to hide her own tears, for her grandfather's sake, but she could not, so finally she let them flow unashamedly. The mourners were gathering outside. Word had gone out all through the mountain cities and towns of Ephraim that Ehud, their righteous judge for eighty years now, lay on his deathbed in Ramah.

She lit the wicks of the many lamps she had made to brighten the room for her almost-blind grandfather. Even though it was long after sunset, the room glowed with a brightness that was close to that of noonday. She had made the wicks extra thick and double dipped them with beeswax so they would burn longer and brighter than the lamps most of the local women made.

She wiped her grandfather's sweat-laden brow, pulled up the woolen blanket over his thin ribs, and kissed his sunken and wrinkled cheek. "Oh, *Saba*, what will Israel do without you? You have been our light in the darkness for so long. I fear the people will not listen to hear the voice of *Adonai* if you're not here to remind them."

Ehud patted her hand and pulled it to his lips. "Listen to me, my dearest little Bee," he gasped with effort, "You must become their light. As an *eschet lapidot,* you must make them understand the light of God. The Lord God will not be mocked. They must listen to His word, and obey, or the consequences will be severe."

"Me?" Deborah quaked. "A woman of light? Why would anyone listen to me? I'm a nobody. I'm only a woman, married to a poor man. I can't be a light! I'm a little bee, remember. I buzz around, making lots of noise that nobody pays any attention to. Besides, the people already have Shamgar ben Anat as a judge, if only they will heed his words. I've heard he killed over six hundred Philistines with only an ox goad. Surely they are more likely to listen to him!"

"No," the old man choked as he struggled to speak, "Shamgar's time is almost at an end. I've already had a word from *Adonai.* You must begin to prepare your husband and yourself. Promise me. You can whisper your judgments into Barak's ear. I will speak to the elders of Ephraim. They will let you teach in the city gate if I tell them to. You know the law as well as any of the men of Bethel or Ramah. You've been by my side as I taught, almost since the day you were born. I know that it's not usual, but with your mother dying so soon after you were born, it was left up to me to raise you, and I couldn't bear to let you out of my sight."

Deborah knelt beside the multi-pillowed pallet and laid her head beside his. "Oh, *Saba,* you know they will never allow any of that. It doesn't matter that I know the law. I'm a woman. They will never let me sit in the city gate and judge as you did, even if I try to hide it by whispering into Barak's ear. They will burn me alive for blasphemy if I even try to speak the words of *Adonai.* They'll say 'her pride has made her mad'."

Ehud laughed, but it came out more like coughing. He frowned. "Well, that may be true, Little Bee, and pride is certainly a pitfall you must avoid at all cost," he warned. "But *Adonai* will protect those He calls. You are called. That's one reason we named you Deborah, the little bee. A bee's honey is sweet, but its sting is painful, even able to kill some men. Other bees may swarm to their leader, but they're all small and vulnerable, so they must never give in to the sin of pride."

He took her small right hand in his huge left one. The left was his arm of strength, if such could even be said any more. Once that arm had slain a king. Now it could barely lift her hand. "You are no longer poor, you know. All I had is now yours. You will be a judge. *Adonai* has decreed it, so it is settled. Call in the elders now. I must speak with them. My time is short. *Adonai* calls to me. I must go home."

Deborah called in the elders and, for Ehud's sake, they all pretended to listen to the old man's vision and consider it. But they had no intention of listening to a young woman, a poor one at that, and letting her tell them how to conduct their business, much less settle their disputes. Nevertheless, Deborah began to prepare for the battle that was sure to come.

CHAPTER 2

*Then the sons of Israel again did evil in the sight of the Lord,
after Ehud died. Judges 4:1*

Barak hurried out into the courtyard of the large house. Deborah bent over a large washtub. "What are you doing out here, wife? The mourners are all gathered. Don't you wish to say goodbye to your grandfather? The hillside is full of people. I didn't even have to hire any of the usual old hens looking for a hand out. They're here, but their tears are genuine, and they never asked for a mite. Do you not wish to show *Saba* the same respect? I know you spent all night washing and wrapping him with spices and the burial cloths, and you must be exhausted, but someone has to stay with him at all times until we take him to his burial cave."

Deborah stood up. She slid her arms into Barak's ripped tunic, wrapped her strong arms around his bared muscular chest, and hugged him tightly. She wasn't a small woman, being nearly as tall as he was; only much thinner. Dark eyes and small lips gave her a kind of beauty that many men wouldn't recognize, but he still quivered with excitement after almost ten years of marriage. Her deep, resonant voice could command attention when she wanted it to, but she didn't recognize that power. Most of the time she spoke so softly that he had to lean closer to hear her. It was only when she sang that everyone would hear and stop to listen to the sweet honey of her song.

"Oh, husband," she whispered against his shoulder, "Someone is with *Saba*. I wouldn't leave him alone. You know that. Yes, I'm tired, but I'll be fine. I just needed to be alone for a while. Everyone keeps urging me to cry. I've already shed enough tears to fill the Sea of Chinnereth, and *Saba* was here then to see me shed them. Tears now are only for my own benefit to cleanse my soul of its longing to have my *Saba* back."

She looked up, tears glistening in her dark eyes despite her words. "He is in the hands of *Adonai* now, and truly, can you think of any more wonderful place to be than with Father Abraham, Father Isaac, Father Jacob, and with his own father and my mother? I have this picture of it in my head with green mountainsides and clear blue skies and the sound of harps and flutes and all kinds of melodies filling the air with an unending song, but somehow I know that it must be even more beautiful than I can imagine. It must be so wonderful there. I wish I could be there with them to see how beautiful it truly is."

Deborah sighed and started to bend back to her work, but he held her upright.

He took her small chin in his hand, and stared into her eyes. "Don't talk such foolishness, woman. Don't you know that I need you here, and so do our little fawns. Remember our four daughters waiting for us at home back in Kedesh. They need their mother as much as I need my wife. I'll hear no more talk of being with our forefathers."

Deborah played with the ripped edge of his mourning garment. "Does it bother you, beloved, that we have only daughters? I know some men would have divorced me long before now."

He lifted her chin and gently kissed the tip of her nose. "Am I that foolish that you would ask me such a question? Am I not treated like a king when I walk through my door with my beautiful angels surrounding me with their kisses and hugs? How could a man not be overwhelmed by such adoration? What more could sons give me?"

He laughed again. "Besides, your *Saba* told me that Jacob's prophecy to Naphtali was about you; 'a hind let loose who has beautiful fawns.' What man can argue with Father Jacob?"

She rubbed her hand down his smooth face that had already been shaved as a sign of mourning for Ehud. "Maybe a man can't, but I think I will ask our Father in Heaven if He can make an exception and give us a beautiful son this time."

He gazed into her dark eyes. "Are you trying to tell me something, wife?"

She shrugged and grinned. "Maybe. But let's not say anything about it at the moment. This is not the time for it. There's too much to do right now."

With these words, she plopped back down beside the huge wooden vat she had used as a washtub since she was a small girl.

"Speaking of which..." He bent down beside her and ran his hand through the mineral salt-whitened water in the tub. "What are you doing here that's so important you would miss your grandfather's funeral lament?"

She stood and wiped her hands on the cloth tied about her waist. "I'm not going to miss it. I'm coming right now. I just wanted to put these wicks in to soak before I left."

He stood, too, and wiped his own hands on the cloth. "Wicks? You're making wicks? Why? Why do you need any more right now? Your grandfather is gone, and we're going home in a few days. Aren't there enough in the lamps to last until then?"

"These aren't for here. My grandfather gave me an idea. He said I was to be an *eschet lapidot*, a woman of light for the people. When *Saba* had so much trouble seeing in the dim light of the oil lamps, I made wicks for the lamps that were brighter and burned longer than most wicks by braiding together three wicks and then soaking them in this salt solution. After they're dried, I'll dip them in the beeswax several times and dry them again…"

Had her *Saba*'s death driven her to madness? Why would she be wasting her time with wicks at a time like this? "What does any of this have to do with…?"

"Don't you see? You can sell my wicks to the tabernacle at Shiloh on our way home. We would want to stop by there anyway to make an offering of thanksgiving for the life of Ehud, my beloved *Saba*. When the priests see how much better my wicks are than the ones they're using now, they will want to use them all the time, and you will be rich."

He scratched his head and laughed. "So, your grandfather told you to be a woman of light to the people, and you took that to mean you're supposed to make better torches? I don't think that's what Ehud meant at all, Deborah. He meant for you to…"

"No, no! You still don't see. He said we both needed to prepare ourselves. He said *Adonai* has something wonderful in mind for both of us. We are both to be the next judges of Israel."

"Judges?! Now I know you've lost your senses! I'm a poor man. No one is going to listen to me! Why would they? Look, I know Ehud left this place to you, and I know by law it's mine since women can't own property, but I would never take your land. If you can find a way to keep it, we can use it as a second home for when we travel back down here to Ephraim."

"Exactly! Now you're beginning to see! We will be doing a lot of traveling back and forth. So, the first thing we have to do is change the way the people look at you. We must buy you some brightly colored robes made of fine linen or silk; the kind that have sleeves in them and tie with cloth sashes instead of these rough ropes. Then they will no longer see you as a poor man. You will be Lappidoth, the man of the torches. We will make the best torches in all of Israel. Everyone will come to us for these wicks."

She gave him a quick kiss. "But first, let us go and bury my grandfather."

CHAPTER 3

But you shall remember the Lord your God, for it is He who is giving you power to make wealth, that He may confirm His covenant which He swore to your fathers, as it is to this day. Deuteronomy 8:18

The elders gathered in Ehud's courtyard. Its cool breezes were normally such a beautiful place of refuge to Deborah. Colorful and fragrant narcissuses, irises, lilies, and cyclamen grew in profusion at their appointed times. Today, however, there was no peacefulness as she hid herself behind the large cedar tree near the house.

Barak looked magnificent. She had dressed him in one of Ehud's fine robes these men had never seen before. They had bought it on their last trip together, right after her youngest daughter was born, and Ehud had become ill not long after they had returned. Barak looked confident. Already he seemed to realize that now he was the master of this household, and someone to be reckoned with. His face glowed in the bright sunlight.

"You all heard what Ehud said," Barak thundered at them. "Deborah is to be the new judge of Israel. *Adonai* has decreed it!"

The elders, a bunch of withered old merchants who had indulged themselves in too much of their own food and wine, all leaned back into Ehud's thick cushions and laughed into their folded hands and sleeved silk cloaks. Only their spokesman, Sair, a fat old wine merchant Deborah had known all her life, stood and faced Barak.

Sair was nice enough to the wealthier men of the town, but made little pretense of civility to its poorer citizens, and none at all to women or children. He had kicked and struck his own wives and children so hard he left dark bruises or welts and once even broke teeth. But since the elders were here now, and a few of them actually liked Barak and wanted to curry his favor, now that he was no longer poor, Sair seemed to be trying to at least appear to listen to him.

"You have to understand, Barak. He was an old man, always more than a bit foolish when it came to that girl. And he must have been out of his mind with the pain of his impending death. We're not listening to such nonsense. Why should we? Things are good just the way they are right now. We don't need any judge, much less a prideful arrogant woman who thinks she can speak for God Almighty." He talked with a mouth full of dates, and now spat out their seeds on the ground, and slouched back into Ehud's favorite cushions in the shade of the sycamore tree.

Even a few of the elders seemed offended by his rudeness. But, though they might not agree with the severity of his wording, they still agreed with his sentiment, for one by one they added their assent to his reasoning.

"My wife is neither prideful nor arrogant," Barak insisted, balling his fists into knots, flexing his fingers, and then balling them again. "She knows quite well your stubbornness and that you would never take heed of her words. She would speak through me just as Moses spoke through his brother Aaron. She wouldn't even have to be seen by the people. We could set up a tent where she could sit and hear the cases and all judgments would come through me. Ehud said *Adonai* had called us as a team."

He folded his hands behind him and paced. "Don't you understand that *Adonai* will have His way? If you do not listen to Ehud's warning, there could be consequences for our nation that would not be good for any of you!"

Sair again rose to his feet. Though Barak was the taller of the two, Sair was more than twice his weight. "Don't you dare threaten us, you peasant!"

Barak was outwardly calm, but he had to be inwardly seething. "I wasn't threatening anything. I was merely reminding you that sometimes *Adonai*'s way of getting us to listen to His commands can be painful and our suffering can be severe if we will not hear."

"And you think His blessings are on you and your wife? Hah! If it weren't for Ehud's legacy, you wouldn't even have a roof over your head tonight. I'd no more listen to your pitiful judgment than I would your fool wife!"

Deborah burst into their sight, and pointed her finger right at Sair's long, bulbous nose. "You are so wrong about my husband! You can make fun of me all you want but Barak of Kedesh, son of Abinoam, is a good man. Far better than you or any one of you here."

Barak put his hands on her shoulders and she took a deep breath. "I will make a deal with you, Sair. There are many more important blessings from *Adonai* than just financial, but because we know money is the only one you would recognize, we will prove to you that the blessings of *Adonai* are on us. If, by this time next year, Barak is not the wealthiest man in this village, we will never speak of any of this again. But if he is, then you will let us judge in the gate just as my *Saba* decreed."

She dropped her finger and lowered her head. *Saba* had warned her about foolish pride.

Sair spat out more seeds. "I don't make deals with women, but I guess I can make that one with this peasant husband of yours.

Everybody here knows I'm the wealthiest man in this village, probably in this part of the country, so if you think you can whip me, go ahead and try. But don't count on ever being able to sit in that gate! It isn't going to happen."

These men were defying the word of *Adonai* from Ehud's lips. Before Barak could stop her, Deborah spoke again, this time wagging her finger at all of them. "Then you had best be prepared for the consequences. *Adonai* has spoken. You did not listen. His favor has been withdrawn from His people. Be assured, God is not mocked. Sooner or later, His judgments are sure to come down on you like rain."

"Yeah, right, woman. You see, Barak, you couldn't even control your wife for one evening. You think we could trust you to control her as a judge? Never! Not while I'm alive, you won't!"

CHAPTER 4

Then he placed the lampstand in the tent of meeting, opposite the table, on the south side of the tabernacle. He lighted the lamps before the Lord, just as the Lord had commanded Moses. Exodus 40:24-25

Deborah waited in the wagon. She had, of course, seen the Tabernacle many times with her grandfather, though she'd never been inside. Since it had been here at Shiloh, the tent had been covered by a mud-brick building to protect it from the unpredictable mountain weather. It was a massive structure compared to all the simple huts and market stalls in the area. Only a few wealthy merchants had homes anywhere near approaching its size. Still, it was a rather simple building, rectangular in shape, and without any great beauty to speak of. She had seen much more ornate buildings in her travels with Ehud.

Out here in the courtyard though was another story. This was a marketplace akin to that of any great city. People were everywhere, some in finery fit for kings, some in rags barely held together with tattered ropes. Merchants sold rams and lambs, red heifers and turtledoves, so the noise and the stench were almost unbearable. A few of the more faithful Rabbis tried to hold court and faithfully teach the laws of Moses. But most of the groups of men that gathered were more interested in the state of their crops or the latest news on the conquests of Jabin II, the king of Hazor, who was terrorizing some of their neighbors to the north though he hadn't yet dared to enter Israel.

There were also many women in the courtyard waiting for a family member to come out from the Tabernacle after making their sacrifices. Some of these were making their own prayers for strong sons or a good husband. But, like the men, most were just gossiping about whatever the topic of the moment might be. One topic was that there were a couple of rather brazen harlots soliciting business out near the gate where those more interested in politics than sacrifice might see them but where they might be safer from the more religiously minded. Deborah lowered her eyes and began to pray for them. Most of these women had had no real choice in the matter. They had been cast aside by the men in their lives, usually for no more reason than that they gave birth to daughters, or were no longer young enough, or pretty enough, or whatever-enough to please a swine of a husband. These poor women were then left to fend for themselves, and often for their children, with no way to do so but harlotry.

Barak came rushing out and climbed up into the wagon, his smooth face red with excitement. "You were so right, wife. Eli, the young priest, loved your wicks! He said they were much better than the ones they've been using. Apparently, the old ones tend to go out even when they're properly trimmed if they're not constantly watched."

He showed her a fistful of gold *shekels*. "He took the whole lot, and said this would pay for an equal number more, but that he would gladly take as many as we could bring him. And he said you made them the perfect lengths for the lampstand and for all of his regular oil lamps. How did you know how to do it? Women aren't allowed in that part of the tabernacle, so I know you've never seen it."

"That part was easy. The lampstand was made from a talent of pure gold with a single shaft in the middle and three branches with almond-shaped blossom and cups on each side. I've heard *Saba* describe it so many times, I'm sure I know exactly what it looks like. I'd say it's at least a cubit and a half wide and maybe two cubits tall."

"Well I certainly didn't take my arm and measure it, but I'd say that's it or mighty close to it." He flicked the reins to move the donkey forward. "Come on, let's go home. Our girls miss their mother."

She shook her head and gathered her robe tighter around her. "No, not yet. We have a stop to make on the way first. I've heard that there's an olive grove not too far from Jerusalem that's for sale, and we're going to buy it."

He stared. "What? Why? Do you know anything about growing olives?"

"Actually, more than you might think. Olive trees are one of the heartiest trees we have in Israel. Some of our trees are said to be many hundreds of years old." At his arched eyebrow, she laughed. "One of the advantages of being Ehud's granddaughter was that I got to hear a lot about some things and a little bit about most everything. This grove is on a mountainside, and it's meant for us to have it. It's said that some of the trees in this grove are close to a thousand years old."

"But Jerusalem is in the wrong direction. Wouldn't it be better to find something nearer to home?"

She shook her head. "No, this is the one. Trust me, my husband. It is as I told Sair. At this time next year, you will be a very wealthy man."

Barak laughed. "Who am I to argue with that? Let's go buy an olive grove, although I still can't figure out why."

"Sure you can, my dearest. We need oil for the lamps. Why should anyone who buys the wicks from us have to buy the oil from someone else?"

"But don't you think we're moving too fast?"

"No, this is not our timing, it's *Adonai*'s. Between the money you made today and the money Ehud left us, we can afford to buy the grove, and I heard from one of the women in the courtyard that it's selling for far less than its value, and that since this past year was its Sabbatical year, we will have six years to harvest before it has another Sabbatical year. That's why we have to get there fast. Do you think it was a coincidence that I overheard her talking about an olive grove in Jerusalem right when I was wondering where we could get oil for our lamps? No, it was an answer to my prayer."

CHAPTER 5

And the Lord sold them into the hand of Jabin king of Canaan, who reigned in Hazor. Judges 4:2a

When they pulled into their hometown, Kedesh was abuzz with the news. Jabin II had a new commander named Sisera, and he was said to be a giant of a man with a voice that could topple trees and strike men dead with fear without him even laying a blade on them. The people quivered with dread. The people of Israel hadn't been so afraid since the ten spies had brought back their report about the Anakim in the Promised Land. Hadn't they learned anything at all from their forty years of wandering in the wilderness? Of course, no one alive today had ever experienced such a thing personally, but surely they had all heard the stories from their grandfathers who heard it from their fathers and grandfathers.

Saba had always made it seem so real, she could taste the honey of the manna, and the overwhelming joy of the sight of the heavy clusters of grapes and the huge pomegranates and all the dates and olives of their new land. She sighed. Some would never learn that their *Adonai* was a God of Might who could take on any enemy, no matter what size or how strong a voice he had. She needed to get home to her girls and reassure them they had nothing to fear.

Their home here was nowhere near as large or as fancy as Ehud's home. It was a simple mud-brick structure with similar homes almost up against it on each side. Cut out windows allowed a breeze in the evenings and a large blanket served as the door. Most of the cooking took place outside at the back of the house on a grate in a large iron oven or in a pot suspended over an open fire. Still, the first sighting of the little home sent a shiver of pleasure up her spine, and she urged Barak to drive faster.

She had first come here as a young bride with Barak. She had been so blessed by *Adonai* in a strong young husband who was kind and considerate of her shyness and her ineptitude at the womanly chores most women learned at their mother's knee. She had known a few basics of sewing and could boil water and make a simple stew, but that was about it. Ehud had always had plenty of servants, and he had preferred having her with him. She knew the law of Moses, as well as the code of Hammurabi, and could even read in both Hebrew and Phoenician, although *Saba* had warned her not to reveal that to anyone but her husband, and then only after they were already married. Those were definitely not qualities to be desired in a wife.

Naturally, her marriage had been arranged. She was older than most when she married: already considered a spinster by the community at sixteen. Ehud had promised her mother that he would only marry her to someone from the tribe of Naphtali, and there weren't many men of Naphtali to be found in Ephraim. The townspeople said the fact that Barak had come to visit the Judge of Ephraim at a time when Ehud despaired of finding a husband for his aging granddaughter was an unfortunate coincidence for her since he was such a poor man. But Deborah didn't agree with them at all. *Adonai* had sent her the perfect mate in answer to Ehud's fervent prayers.

Barak was still so handsome, with his twinkly brown eyes and a ruddy complexion that threatened to blush at the most inconvenient times and a mouth that kept a huge smile more often than not. When they married, he was only twenty, quite young to be a widower, the wife of his youth having died in childbirth along with the babe. He was kind to a fault. It was obvious the women of Kedesh adored him, his lack of wealth notwithstanding, and they had been more than a little dismayed when he brought home a new bride from Ephraim. Nevertheless, Deborah had found welcome in the community. It earned its reputation as a city of refuge by its true hospitality, and in a short time, the women had granted her access to their midst.

"*Ima! Abba! Ima, Abba,* you're home!" Four little girls came running out of the house, shouting as they ran. Rachel, the oldest, of course led the procession, followed closely by the twins Sarah and Rebecca. Little three-year-old Tamar toddled further back with her arms extended for her daddy to pick her up and swing her around like he did every time he came home to them. She wasn't disappointed. Soon Barak had all four girls up in his arms and twirled them again and again until they were dissolving in fits of giggles and had rained so many kisses on his beardless face, he too was laughing like a madman. Barak's mother finally appeared, wiping her hands on her apron and hugging her son.

It was little Tamar who suddenly changed the mood. "*Abba,*" she stroked his cheek, "where's your beard? Your face is so scratchy. Why did you take away all my lovely curls? And your tunic is torn! *Ima, Safta* Mara. *Abba* tore his tunic!"

Barak handed Tamar over to Deborah, and they both hugged all the girls. "Don't worry, my little angels. My beard will soon grow back. I had to shave it and tear my tunic to show respect. Your *Saba* Ehud died and he's now in Abraham's bosom with Father Isaac, and Father Jacob and with all your other *Saba*s and *Safta*s. Do you all understand that?"

The older girls slowly nodded, but Tamar shook her head vehemently. "Will he come back soon? I don't want him to go anywhere!"

She laid her head onto Deborah's chest and sobbed violently. All the girls soon had tears running down their cheeks.

"It's okay," Barak told them. "Go ahead and cry. It's good for you to show how much you loved your *Saba*. I know how much you'll miss him. *Adonai* never gets angry with us for showing Him our grief. No, *Saba* won't be coming back to join us here, but someday we'll all go to join him. *Adonai* has a special place waiting for us in *Sheol* with all those who are faithful. When we die, we are gathered to our people. Won't that be a great reunion? And you know what? *Safta* Leah, *Saba*'s wife is there too. You never met her, but I'll bet *Saba* is so excited to see her and to tell her how glad he is to be there with her after so long. You wouldn't want to deny him the pleasure of being with his beloved, now would you?"

The older girls agreed they wouldn't, but little Tamar still wasn't convinced. Barak took her in his arms and comforted her until she finally fell asleep.

Since it was nearing the breeze before the setting sun, Deborah insisted that her mother-in-law take a break and enjoy being with Barak and the girls, and she swiftly set about making dinner. She had learned a lot about cooking in the past ten years, and soon had a light soup of leeks and lentils, a dish of cucumbers, olives and onions in a pomegranate wine sauce, and breads and cheeses prepared for her family. She'd even brought home honey cakes and fig jam as a special treat. The girls were ecstatic. *Safta* Mara took excellent care of the girls, and kept an immaculate house, but she wasn't really much of a cook. Barak always said that was why he'd never complained about Deborah's cooking. To him it was heavenly. His *Ima* burned butter.

CHAPTER 6

You shall not covet your neighbor's house; you shall not covet your neighbor's wife or his male servant or his female servant or his ox or his donkey or anything that belongs to your neighbor. Exodus 20:17

The morning found Deborah stooped over the foul smelling pot retching violently.

"So, that's the way of it!"

She looked up. Mara stood behind her, grimace-faced.

"Have you told Barak yet?"

"Yes, he knows." She wiped her mouth with a rag she had dipped into her washbowl.

"So when do you expect this girl to come?"

"Hopefully by the barley harvest, but it isn't a girl. I can tell. It feels different than it's ever felt before. I've never even had morning sickness before, not even with the twins. You know that."

"That doesn't mean a thing. Three times before I've prayed for a man-child to take away the disgrace from this family brought on by my husband Abinoam's fondness for wine. *Adonai* never once listened to my prayer. It's probably just the onions you put in the soup last night. Onions always made me retch the next morning."

Deborah straightened and arched her back. "Ah, but you had only boys. I ate onions all the time with my girls and I never retched from it."

"Just don't get your hopes up. Women who have girls tend to always have girls, you know. That's why they're considered barren, and their husbands divorce them."

Deborah gazed at her steadily. "Yes, and they generally marry other women who also have girls. Doesn't that tell you something?"

Mara raised her hand to strike Deborah. "Are you saying this is Barak's fault? How dare you? Why, I should tell him you're an ungrateful..."

Deborah backed away, her eyes gleaming with astonishment. She and her mother-in-law had never had cross words before. Mara had always been kind to her. "*Ima* Mara, I wasn't saying any such thing. There is no fault in having a girl. That's all I was saying. I love Barak and my girls with all my heart. I wouldn't change them if I could. I believe all our children are gifts from *Adonai*, and they're wonderful gifts whether they're boys or girls. I just believe this time I'm having a boy."

Piercing screams interrupted any further discussion. Both women ran toward them.

"It's mine!" Jael, a little girl who lived next door, grabbed at Rachel's hair and yanked.

Rachel screamed again, and jerked around, landing a blow to the other girl's cheek. "No, it's mine! I found it!"

Rachel ran to hide behind Deborah from the sure retaliation.

Jael held her hand to her reddening cheek. Jael's mother came running out of her house. "Give it back! You know it's mine! *Ima*, tell them it's mine! My *dohd* gave it to me for my weaning celebration. I've had it ever since."

Jael began to cry.

"Girls, girls, calm down!" Deborah separated the girls with her outspread arms. "What's going on here? Why are you two fighting? You've always been such good friends."

"She stole my alabaster hair comb!" Jael accused. She made another grab for the comb, but Rachel hid herself even further behind Deborah's back.

Rachel stuck her head out only enough to speak. "I did not! I found it! It's mine now!"

Deborah pulled Rachel from behind her, and made her face her. "Wait, Rachel, you said it was yours now. So you admit you knew it was Jael's?"

Rachel lowered her face. "Yes, but I didn't steal it. I found it under our tree. She must have left it there. She abandoned it like it was worthless to her. That makes it mine now." Grinning smugly, she added, "That's the law."

Jael renewed her efforts to get at Rachel. "I've been looking for it for days, haven't I, *Ima*?" Her mother nodded vigorously, but said nothing. "I'd given up hope of ever finding it again, but it's still mine! I don't care what your stupid law says!"

Deborah held up her hands to quiet each of them. "Wait just a moment, Jael. You may care more than you think what the law actually says. When did you find it, Rachel?"

Rachel hung her head, but Deborah lifted her chin. "I asked when you found it, daughter."

Rachel bit her lower lip. "I found it last *Shabbat*."

Rachel's eyes were closed. She couldn't look Deborah in the eyes, a sure sign she was hiding something. "And you hid it, didn't you, not daring to wear it for almost a week, thinking that if you waited, the law of abandonment would work in your favor. You coveted Jael's comb, and you failed to do her the *mitzvah* of returning what you knew was her property. Give Jael her comb right now!"

Rachel sighed, but handed over the comb. Deborah held her daughter's shoulder. Rachel was tall for her age, and slender like

Deborah, but she had more her father's coloring and his big brown eyes. She was developing into quite a beauty. It would not be too many years now before a *mohar* would be paid, and she would be betrothed. Deborah just wanted to be sure that before that happened, she had been taught the true law of *Adonai*, a law of kindness and respect. "As a punishment, every day until the new moon, you will go over to Jael's house and comb her hair for her before bedtime, and if I find out you have pulled her hair or harmed her in any way, you'd best beware of my wrath. Do you understand? Now go inside and plead for *Adonai*'s forgiveness for your covetousness."

After Rachel had gone in, and her *Ima* Shachar had sent Jael inside their own house, Deborah, Shachar, and Mara stood under the tree where Rachel said the comb had been found.

"Jael isn't usually so careless with her comb," Shachar sighed. "But I know Rachel wouldn't take it either."

"Thank you for believing that, Shachar. Although you wouldn't know it by her behavior this morning, Rachel is usually a very kind and loving child. I've never before known her to take anything that didn't belong to her."

"And she didn't this time either," Mara pointed. "Look here in all this underbrush. That's the wooden cooking spoon I've been looking for all week and I'll bet that's the axe head I heard your husband fussing about, Shachar!"

"It is! Oh, Saul will be so pleased we found that! He was so upset it was gone! I wonder how all this stuff got here. Wait, I know! That windstorm that blew through last week! I'll bet it just picked up anything in its path, but the tree knocked them back to the ground, and the wind covered them with leaves. It could have been summer before we found them, and by then none of it would have been any good. That must have been some windstorm to pick up an axe head!"

"You'd be amazed what the wind can do," Deborah agreed. "It's a good thing that axe head only hit the tree. If it hit a person, it could have killed them."

"I know," Shachar nodded. "We definitely wouldn't want that to happen." She leaned forward and whispered, "Not again! That's why Saul and I came here to this city of refuge. We're Kenites, and our home is far south of here. Our ox gored a man. It was an accident, and we were cleared of any wrongdoing, but we were told we should run before his family came to kill us. There are other cities of refuge closer to home, but we wanted to get as far away from home as possible. We've never told anybody here that. We even changed our names. We were afraid to trust anyone. But I do trust you, Deborah. Most women would have taken their daughter's side, regardless of the truth. I might have myself."

"No you wouldn't, Shachar. And that's a beautiful name! Dawn. That's my favorite time of the day. A new beginning, just like you have here! You're a good woman. Your husband seems to be a good man, and I know you're both raising your daughter to be the same."

"Jael is all we have. We had a son, but he died as a small child when a sickness swept through the town. It was only a week after his weaning celebration. I think that's why my brother gave Jael such a valuable comb for her celebration, and maybe why Jael is so attached to it. It's a reminder of the older brother she never knew."

Deborah and Mara both gave Shachar a hug.

"Then it's very good that she has her comb back." Deborah looked toward the house. "If you don't mind, I'll tell that to Rachel. I know then she'll truly want to apologize to Jael. She really does have a tender heart. She would never have kept the comb if she had known how much it meant to Jael."

"Thank you. Deborah, you're really good at solving problems. Certainly you may tell Rachel." She cocked her head sideways and scratched the back of her hand. "You know the law, right?"

Deborah nodded. "Yes, my *Saba* was Ehud, the judge of Israel. He began teaching me the law before I could walk. Why?"

"My sister-in-law, Zayith, came here with us since she was unmarried at the time, but she has since married a man from the tribe of Issachar. *Adonai* has greatly blessed her in her marriage, but she has this neighbor..."

CHAPTER 7

Now Deborah, a prophetess, the wife of Lappidoth, was judging Israel at that time. Judges 4:4

And so it began. Barak teased her that *Adonai* could even use a randy rooster to accomplish His will to make Deborah a judge in Israel.

Shachar's sister-in-law raised chickens, and her neighbor had a rooster who was constantly getting into her hen house, no matter what Zayith or her neighbor did to keep him out. The neighbor demanded that Zayith pay her for his "services," even though Zayith hadn't asked for them. She had her own rooster, although the neighbor claimed that Zayith's rooster was the direct result of her own rooster, and therefore she should be paid for his services too.

Deborah agreed to listen to both sides and give her opinion, although she warned Shachar that she couldn't guarantee that she would rule in Zayith's favor. In the end, Deborah had worked out a deal to let both women share the services of both roosters since it seemed that the problem was the older rooster was neglecting his own hens in favor of Zayith's.

After that, it was only a matter of weeks before more and more women came with their problems. Deborah couldn't have all these people coming to her home. It wasn't big enough, and all the noise upset her neighbors and her own children. She had to find a place to meet with them. As she prayed one evening, *Adonai* told her to go to the palm grove outside of town.

Word got around that Deborah was holding court twice a week out under the palm trees not far from Kedesh. It would have been much easier in the city gate but, of course, the elders of Kedesh were no more amenable to that idea than the elders of Ephraim had been. There was a good side to the decision to hold court under the palm trees though: *Adonai* had driven away all the temple priestesses and prostitutes that used to hold their pagan ceremonies and rituals out there. Deborah hadn't had to lift a finger. Instead, she had lifted her voice in prayer and praise as she anointed every tree with pure olive oil and fragrant myrrh and asked *Adonai* to drive out the demons and evil spirits and to stand guard that they might never be allowed back in. Of course, that meant a few plaintiffs had turned aside too, but Deborah had all the cases she could handle, especially in her now-visible condition.

For a good while, all her cases had been women and children. She could see why Shachar had been surprised that she hadn't automatically sided with her daughter Rachel concerning Jael's comb. In almost every case where a child was involved, the mothers had gotten involved too, and had escalated the problem. Left on their own, in most cases the children could have worked out their differences.

Hopefully, this case would be exactly like that. Except, these boys were now considered men in the eyes of the law. They had both had their *bar mitzvah* only a week ago. Joshua was the older of the two. He was dressed in a plain white tunic and linen turban, and his bulky physique and rough hairy face, even at such a young age, said he should have been named Esau. But his soft voice and gentle demeanor told Deborah that wouldn't have been a good name for him at all. No, that "honor" belonged to the smaller, wiry boy, inappropriately named Jacob. Deborah had observed Jacob taunting Joshua at every opportunity as she had heard other cases. Jacob was dressed in a fine linen, almost a festal robe, and was as bejeweled as a peacock, and as they came forward, he almost strutted like one too.

"Why have you come here today?"

Both mothers tried to answer at once.

"Please, I'd like to hear it from your sons."

"He stole my wife," Jacob complained loudly. "And I want her back. He's such a shmuck he wouldn't be able to satisfy her anyway!"

"Young man, you will not talk that way here if you want a judgment from me!"

Jacob glared at her defiantly. "Well, I don't particularly. My *Ima* insisted we come here, but you have no authority. Why should I respect a judgment from you?"

"I don't know. You're right. I have no authority except from *Adonai*, but I do know the law. Do you want a chance to get your bride back, or not?"

"Of course I do," he muttered.

Deborah held her hand out for Joshua to speak. "What do you have to say about this, Joshua?"

His voice was so soft, Deborah had to strain to hear him. "I'm sorry Jacob's mad. *Ima* and *Abba* knew I liked Chesed, so they arranged the marriage for us. I didn't know anything about any arrangement for Jacob to have her."

"Have you come together yet?"

"No. *Abba* only paid the *mohar* a couple of weeks ago. My *Abba* and I just started building the addition to our house. It will probably be at least the Sukkoth festival before *Abba* prepares the wedding feast and sends me for Chesed."

Deborah nodded. That was all exactly according to Jewish traditions. Joshua had up to one year to claim his bride, although they were already considered married under the law. "So Jacob, why do you think Chesed is your bride?"

"It's been agreed since we were children she would be."

"I see. Had a *mohar* been paid?"

"No, but *Abba* was going to pay it last week at my *bar mitzvah*. When he went to pay, Chesed's *Abba* told him Chesed was already pledged to Joshua."

"Did Chesed's *Abba* give your *Abba* any reason for his decision?"

"No, not that I know of. " He glanced at his mother, who shook her head sadly. "Can I have my wife back now?" His voice was almost whiney like that of baby Tamar when she needed a nap.

"No." She explained the law to him as clearly as possible. "You have no case against Joshua. He legally married Chesed, and he didn't wrong you in any way. But your *Abba* may have a case against Chesed's *Abba*. That is, if they want to pursue this further. Although the *mohar* had not yet been paid, if there was an understanding between them, the marriage agreement should not have been broken without cause and your *Abba* should have been informed and given the chance to pay the *mohar*."

"So *Abba* can come back here, and then I can have Chesed?" Again, Jacob reminded her of a toddler demanding his own way.

She tried to be firm, but reasonable. "I don't know, Jacob. I would have to hear from your *Abba* and Chesed's *Abba* before I could decide."

CHAPTER 8

The Lord is my strength and song, and He has become my salvation; This is my God, and I will praise Him; My father's God, and I will extol Him.
Exodus 15:2

It seemed to Barak that Deborah's plan to make him the richest man in Ephraim was coming along splendidly. Maybe a little too well. Eli, the young priest, had told everyone about the fabulous new wicks that were lighting up the Tabernacle "with a divine glow like I've never seen before." Barak had so many new orders for wicks Deborah had had to hire half a dozen women from Kedesh. She carefully taught them how to make the wicks, but somehow for most of them, their wicks still didn't turn out as good as Deborah's, and he feared she would exhaust herself trying to keep up with the demand.

They had also hired men from Jerusalem to work the olive grove—not that there was that much to do there yet. It was far too early. The olive trees hadn't even blossomed yet. The problem with olives was that when they were ready, the entire grove had to be picked and pressed immediately. That was a massive job, and already Barak paced back and forth at night trying to figure out where he was going to get enough workers for it. And Deborah wouldn't even be able to help with much of that. The new baby would be coming right around then. It was said that the Israelite women in Egypt had dropped their babies, and gone right back to work in the fields. Deborah was strong, and had worked soon after her babes were born—but not that fast.

As he rode to Ramah to check on the house Ehud had left them, Barak pondered Ehud's prophecy and Ephraim's response to it. While his fortunes had been soaring, the area of Ephraim was already suffering. The spring rains hadn't come until it was too late to do much good. Then it had flooded much of the area.

Barak surveyed the damage; it was far worse than expected. The town well was nothing but a mud hole. It would be useless for quite a while. Most of the vegetation was destroyed. Rotting plants and dead animals everywhere made quite a stench. Most of the mud brick houses were destroyed too. Tents were pitched for the women and children as men worked frantically to rebuild the sections of their homes that were missing or needed to be patched.

"Are you here to gloat?"

"What?" Barak looked around. Sair stood behind him with his arms folded across his chest and a snarl on his florid face. Barak dismounted and took the donkey by its rope. "No, of course not. Why would I?"

"Because it didn't take long. I guess you're already the richest man in Ephraim. The rest of us are ruined. At least I am, and I don't know of anybody else in town who's doing any better."

Slowly, Barak walked the donkey in the direction of Ehud's home. "I'm sorry to hear that. Truly I am. What can I do to help?"

"Tell *Adonai* to call off the drought and the floods." Sair kicked a rock that plopped in a puddle at Barak's feet. "That's what you can do!"

He looked Sair in the eye. "Are you going to let Deborah be a judge in the city gate?"

Sair grunted. "Not while I'm alive, she won't."

Shaking his head, Barak responded, "Then I'm afraid I can't help you. *Adonai* has spoken. Deborah is already fulfilling the prophecy in the palm trees outside of Kedesh. The people are coming to her for her judgments, and she's helping them. She hasn't even needed me to speak for her. If you could see her, you'd…"

"So why isn't she sitting in your city gate then?" Sair growled. "Why would *Adonai* force us to give her what she already has the opportunity to do elsewhere?"

"Because our elders are as foolish as yours are," Barak shrugged. "But I think it may be better that she's where she is, at least for the moment. People are coming from all around Zebulun and Naphtali, not just from Kedesh. But, truthfully, I think that sooner or later, we're going to have to move back to Ramah and I'll go back and forth to Kedesh to do business, just so that more people can come to her. I know you don't understand, Sair, but *Adonai*'s power is strong on Deborah, and the people are listening to what she has to say. More come every day."

Sair was petulant. "Only a bunch of foolish women and children, from what I hear."

Barak shook his head. "No, that was true at first, but now many men have come too. Wives have a way of persuading their husbands to listen when they know *Adonai* has spoken his wisdom, even if it was through a woman."

"That's the problem. I simply don't believe *Adonai* would ever speak through a woman. Why would He? Man was first deceived through a woman. Didn't *Adonai* rebuke Father Adam for listening to the voice of a woman? Does *Adonai* change His mind so easily?"

As they had talked, they had continued to walk slowly, but often stopped to face each other as they made a point. In a way, it rather reminded him of the kind of debates he had had with Ehud when he was alive. He blinked several times as the memory forced him to focus. He had oftentimes found himself on the wrong side of

Ehud's perfect logic. What would Ehud say now? Then it came to him.

"But Father Adam knew that the words his wife spoke contradicted *Adonai*'s own words. Surely that's different. Aren't we to examine all words, whether they are spoken by a man or by a woman, to see if they are in line with *Adonai*'s own words? Then we will be responsible to *Adonai* Himself for our decisions, just as any righteous judge is responsible to *Adonai* for his or her judgments."

For the first time, Sair seemed to question his own point, but he quickly shook it off. "That may be true, but I believe what I believe, and I'm the chief elder of this town, so you'll never get me to change! I think you've been deceived by a clever, but evil woman. Look what's already happened here. She's called down her demons to destroy us. You want proof? I haven't got a grapevine standing, and there isn't a merchant in town whose goods weren't totally ruined by the flooding. But go look at Ehud's house. There's not a brick or a stone missing. It looks just like it did the day you left here. You tell me how that's possible except she used her magic to curse us!"

With that, he strode off in the direction of his own home.

As Barak rounded the corner to Ehud's house, he could easily see why Sair was so skeptical. The big house stood almost majestically in the midst of all the devastation, as if it had indeed been divinely protected from even a droplet of the rain, much less an entire flood. He reached his arm through the hole in the wood door and inserted his wooden key to release the catch. The wood crossbeam slid to its unlocked position, and he pushed the door open. He cautiously entered the house, brought in his provisions and put his donkey into the inner courtyard. Then he returned and inserted the wooden key to relock the door.

He breathed in a lingering fragrance of the spices Deborah had used to prepare Ehud's body. It almost canceled out the stench of the town that floated in even through the blanketed and shuttered windows. After lighting a couple of Deborah's oil lamps and feeding and watering the donkey, Barak went from room to room looking for structural damage. Sair was right. He found none at all. The blankets weren't even moldy.

"Baruch atah Adonai Eloheinu..."

Barak went through every blessing he knew, thanking and praising *Adonai* for His blessing and provision in sparing Ehud's house and legacy. It was much more than just a house to Deborah. It was all she had of Ehud and her mother. Still, even the many ritual blessings he spoke didn't seem enough. How could a few memorized words begin to sum up his deep gratitude? If he could sing like Deborah, he would have burst out in song. Well, why not? He was alone here and there was no one to hear and be offended by his lack of skill at singing.

So he sang. And he sang. And he sang some more. It was the first time in his life he'd ever sung. Tears poured from his eyes as the words poured from his lips. The words weren't from any song he'd ever heard before. They just seemed to flow into his mind and right out his mouth. It was the same way with the music. Maybe it wasn't beautiful, but maybe it wasn't as bad as he'd expected either.

Deborah often made up songs. Some were silly songs to entertain the girls, but most were songs of worship to *Adonai*. He loved to listen to her melodious voice, and always coaxed her to sing for his friends, but he'd never tried to claim such a gift for himself. Only that extreme feeling of gratitude had brought it out in him. It simply couldn't be expressed any other way. *Adonai* had truly blessed them far beyond his own faith. As Deborah had said, olives were extremely hearty, and his orchard was fine. Deborah and the girls were safe and out of harms' way. Ehud's house was a miracle like he'd never experienced before. *Adonai*'s blessings were overwhelming. He was grateful.

Finally, his emotions were spent. Barak said a few more blessings, got a bite to eat, and lay down in Deborah's room to sleep. For some reason he couldn't quite bring himself to sleep in

Ehud's bed. Besides, it made him feel closer to Deborah to breathe in the fragrance of her pillows. Tomorrow was *Shabbat*. He'd have to stay here before going home the first day of the week.

He slept peacefully until almost dawn. Then he heard a loud crash and smelled smoke. He sprang up from the bed and ran to the front room. A curtain of flames blocked his passage. The house was on fire!

CHAPTER 9

The angel of the Lord encamps around those who fear Him, and rescues them. Psalm 34:7

"They tried to kill me, Deborah! They shot a flaming arrow at Ehud's window. When it had burned enough, they threw in an oil lamp to finish the job. I heard it crash. They expected me to be in that room. If I had been, I'd be dead right now! It's amazing to me that I'm not. It was only with the help of a stranger that I escaped with the donkey out through the courtyard. The house and most of its contents are gone. And to think, I'd just been singing and praising *Adonai* for sparing it. Now it looks just like every other hovel in Ramah." Barak paced back and forth, flailing his arms as he continued his tirade.

"We must certainly thank and reward that stranger."

He stopped pacing and stared at Deborah. "I already tried, but he disappeared right afterwards, and no one seemed to know who I was talking about. I described him to several people, but they all said they'd never seen him before. And another odd thing; he called me Lappidoth. I just figured he didn't know my name, but knew that I was the seller of torches. Now I'm not so sure. I liked the name, especially on his lips. Somehow, it made me feel safe with him. After what had happened, why would I have trusted a stranger to help me? But I trusted him. Now I know it was because he knew my secret name."

"Yes," she smiled. "You are Lappidoth tonight. I see the Light of *Adonai* in you stronger than I ever have before. Something about you has changed."

"Maybe it's just the leftover smoke and ashes."

"No, it isn't that at all."

He shrugged. "I don't know. Right now, I don't feel any different. I'm angry with the men who tried to kill me and took away your legacy from Ehud just because they were jealous that *Adonai* had protected your home and destroyed theirs. You didn't do anything to them, and neither did I. Their own stubbornness was their downfall. But they would take away my children's father! Then how would you and the girls survive?"

Deborah had sent the girls to Shachar's as soon as they'd received their *Abba*'s kisses so they wouldn't hear their parents talk and be worried. So now she removed Barak's outer cloak and kneaded his strong shoulders. Mara was helping deliver a babe at the other end of the village. She rained kisses on his ear and neck. "I'm so glad you're safe. That's all I care about."

Mara and Deborah had both been pacing through the day yesterday as they waited for Barak's return. When Barak hadn't returned by nightfall, Deborah had fallen on her face before *Adonai* and begged him to spare her husband. But now, any trace of fear had dissipated.

"*Adonai* would protect your family just as He protected you. Think about it. Why weren't you in Ehud's room? As the master of the house, it was certainly your right. Were you afraid of *Saba*'s spirit? That doesn't sound like you at all."

"No, of course not. I don't know. I think I just wanted to feel closer to you. In your room, I could still smell the fragrance of your hair in your pillows, and I lay there remembering the night the twins were conceived there, and…"

"And perhaps the Spirit of *Adonai* sent you there and gave you sweet dreams to keep you there to protect you. You said earlier you were singing. I've never heard you sing before."

Barak rubbed his short but full beard and pursed his lips. "That's because I've never done it before. I don't know why or how I did then. The words came out of my mouth in a melody that seemed made just for the words. They weren't from any song I'd ever heard, at least not that I remember. And how could they be? I was praising *Adonai* for seeing the miracle of Him sparing Ehud's house when all the others around him were destroyed, and for leaving you a legacy of faith in an all-powerful and all-mighty God.

"If you had seen it, Deborah, you'd understand. All the mud-brick houses all around were falling apart. People were living in tents just like at Sukkoth except that Sukkoth is a time of joy. These people were in despair. A few of the men were working together trying to help each other repair their homes, but I don't know how long it will take, and if it rains again like the old ones say it's going to, the damage is going to keep getting worse. But Ehud's house stood right there in the midst, and there wasn't a damaged brick on it. Even the wooden door and shutters didn't feel at all damp, like the rain had just circled around the house.

"I prayed every prayer I knew, but it wasn't enough. I just felt so overwhelmed, all I could think to do was sing. I've heard you do it so many times, and I've always loved to listen to you, but it had never occurred to me to do it myself. But it was like that night I couldn't not sing! Does that make any sense at all? I'm not sure it does to me."

Deborah wrapped her arms around his neck and climbed onto his lap. "Oh, beloved, it makes perfect sense. The Spirit of *Adonai* was so strong upon you, your heart couldn't hold it in. I think the gift of song is one of His greatest gifts to us. It's the one way our heart communes directly with His heart, and at the same time declares to all around us His glory and majesty and our faith in Who He is."

"But soon after the words were out of my mouth, the reason for my praise was gone. The house is gone, or at least most of it. It's no better off than any of the other houses in Ramah, and if it rains, it may even be worse. Where was *Adonai*'s protection then?"

Deborah laughed. "It was right there on you. You are much more valuable to Him than a house! He sent His angel to get you safely out. He had protected the house just so you would see it and praise Him for Who He is. Once you'd done that, *HaSatan* could have it. *Adonai* needed to know the house isn't an idol to you. He is your God, not a house. And the legacy that Ehud left me could never be contained in mud and brick. It's in my faith in *Adonai*, and my love for you and my children, and even the men who did this terrible thing. That's what Sair and his kind would never understand. We must love *Adonai* for Who He is, not for what He does for us. He gives and takes away, but blessed be He. It's when we learn that lesson that we can be truly at peace no matter what happens."

Suddenly she bent over. "I think your son agrees with me. Want to feel him kick?" She placed his hand on her abdomen. "Feel how much lower down he lies than his sisters? That's why I'm so certain he's a boy."

Barak's smile widened at the sharp kick. "Well, boy or girl, whoever's in there is a good kicker! That's a good thing for the babe, but you must be tired."

"Not so tired I couldn't warmly welcome my husband after his long journey. The girls won't be home until dinner time."

"I see." Gently, he lifted her and carried her to his bed.

CHAPTER 10

But if in the field the man finds the girl who is engaged, and the man forces her and lies with her, then only the man who lies with her shall die.
Deuteronomy 22:25

Deborah stared at the two older men before her. They were both in the long-sleeved, bejeweled garb of the wealthy. It seemed, from the size of their large abdomens, that they had a common love of rich foods. But neither had a countenance of pride or arrogance today. They were plainly both worried. "First, will you tell me your names and why you're here?"

"I'm Micah ben Caleb. You told my boy Jacob I had a case against Chesed's *Abba*. Here he is!"

"I'm David ben Judah," the other agreed. "Chesed is my youngest daughter."

"Frankly, I'm surprised to see you here, gentlemen. Since you didn't come when Joshua and Jacob first came to me, I thought the issue had been settled. What has changed?"

"Jacob has kidnapped Chesed," her father charged.

"No! He didn't kidnap her. He's just taken his lawful bride. Jacob said you told him I had a case, and he could get her back. So he took her."

Deborah flushed. "I said no such thing," she cried. "I told him you both needed to come here and tell me exactly what happened before I could decide anything. He heard what he wanted to hear."

Micah removed his hat and scratched his nearly bald head. "Well, I'll admit Jacob has a tendency to do that, but you did say I had a case; my wife said so too, so it can't be kidnapping. He's only married a wife."

Deborah frowned. Didn't he realize how serious this was? "But Chesed was already legally betrothed to Joshua. The *mohar* had already been paid. If you had come here and we could have settled this perhaps you could have given back Joshua's father his *mohar* and reached an agreement with him before things got to this point."

He twirled the one curl left near his forehead. "Doesn't matter. I'll pay Joshua's father back whatever he paid."

Deborah shook her head vehemently. "You still don't understand! It doesn't work like that, Micah. If you had come here before Jacob took this man's daughter, maybe it could have. Why didn't you?"

"I suppose because David's my friend. We've been friends since we were boys. I didn't want to cause any more problems. Our wives are already at each other's throats. I thought maybe Jacob would just get over it and find someone else to marry. That's what I kept trying to tell him to do. But he didn't, and I don't want my boy accused of nothing like kidnapping. Chesed was promised to him. Why can't he have her?"

Deborah sighed. This wasn't going to be at all easy. Maybe she should start with the root of the problem. "Why did you break your word, David? Would you please tell me that?"

The other man gazed at the ground sheepishly. "I don't really know the answer to that myself. Chesed refused to marry Jacob. She wouldn't tell me why. I didn't want to hurt Jacob or Micah, but

I didn't believe Chesed would refuse to marry Jacob without a cause. She's always been a very level-headed girl."

Micah shrugged, and shifted back and forth from one foot to the other. Deborah could see where Jacob got his immense energy. "That isn't reason enough, is it? See, she should belong to Jacob. Since when does a foolish young girl get to choose who she marries?"

Deborah frowned. "I don't know. If you had come before me as I suggested, I would have asked Chesed to tell me why she didn't want to marry Jacob, and she could have given me her reason. No, young women aren't normally allowed to choose their own husbands, but maybe some marriages would be better if they could, and maybe she did have a good reason. Jacob's rash behavior certainly doesn't preclude that possibility. On the other hand, I didn't really know my husband at all when we married, and *Adonai* has blessed us greatly."

She stepped down from her chair and walked toward the two men. "The problem that you two seem to be forgetting is that Chesed was lawfully betrothed to Joshua. What you don't seem to realize is that if Jacob has lain with her, they could both be liable to stoning, unless Chesed cried out, in which case, only Jacob could be stoned. How long have they been gone, and where were they when you realized they were missing?"

Micah's florid face went ashen, and he clutched his chest. David had to catch him, although he seemed near to fainting himself. At last, Micah was able to speak. "They've been missing since yesterday, and my best camel is missing too."

"We think Chesed was walking down by the river when he took her," David added. "Look here. We found her headscarf and one of her sandals in the mud. See. There is blood on the scarf, so that proves she did fight him."

Deborah felt the dried blood. "That's a good sign for her case," she agreed. "Don't lose that scarf. You may need it as evidence."

CHAPTER 11

She used to sit under the palm tree of Deborah between Ramah and Bethel in the hill country of Ephraim; and the sons of Israel came up to her for judgment. Judges 4:5

"So tell me again, why are we moving to Ramah?" Barak grumbled. "The house is gone, or very close to it. It will take me weeks to repair it and that's only if I can get plenty of help. We have everything we need in Kedesh, and yes, I know, even without Ehud's house, I'm easily the wealthiest man in Ephraim, but the elders of Ramah still aren't going to let you judge in the city gate. You know that!"

She nodded agreement. "Yes, I do know that. It doesn't matter. I've already decided I'm going out under the palm trees up on the mountainside between Ramah and Bethel. It'll be just like it was in Kedesh. It serves a double purpose that way. The palm groves are places of great sexual immorality. It's blasphemous the evil that goes on there in the name of *Baal* and *Ashtoreth*. If I go there in the name of *Adonai*, the evil will stop. HaSatan's demons cannot withstand the presence of *Adonai*. Also, that way I won't need to speak through you as I would in the city gate. The people who will come to me will come because they know that I speak the truth of *Adonai*, and they seek His voice, not mine. There won't be any need for pretense. Besides, *Adonai* has told me that He has other plans for you. You won't have time to play nursemaid to me. You will be a great leader of the people in your own right."

"Oh, really?" He cocked his eyebrow in that way she found so amusing. "And what might those plans be?"

Shrugging, she whispered, so the children wouldn't overhear, "I don't know yet, beloved. For now, we are to keep doing what we've been doing. I do know that it's very important that, as you go from town to town, you make as many friends as possible. You will earn the respect of many, and there will come a time when you will need every friend you have."

Barak chewed on that information for a while, remaining silent as he drove the donkey. "So then, why are we moving to Ramah? The people of Kedesh have accepted you. Even if you're not sitting in the gate, many of the men and even some of the elders come to you for your advice. In Ramah, you'll be starting all over. You'll have to deal with Sair, and I wouldn't be at all surprised to find that he was behind the fire."

She looked back at Mara and the girls. They were all sleeping. "I know. I wouldn't be surprised either, but we don't know that, and I don't know why we have to go right now either. I just know *Adonai* said go."

"But shouldn't we wait at least until after the babe is born?"

"No. *Adonai* said we must hurry. I've already warned Shachar and her family to leave Kedesh immediately. We had to leave today."

It wasn't until several days later that Barak heard the news. King Jabin's forces under Commander Sisera had ravaged Kedesh. Many of the townspeople had been killed or maimed, and many of the women and girls beaten and raped. What many had long feared had now come to pass: Sisera had invaded Israel.

CHAPTER 12

Because Your lovingkindness is better than life,
my lips will praise You. Psalm 63:3

Although word of Sisera's triumph in Kedesh spread like a plague, it didn't change much in Ramah. The people continued with their work of trying to rebuild the town. But *Adonai* also fought against them. The rains kept coming. Every time they thought they were finally making progress, the rains would start again. Even Ehud's house seemed to refuse to be rebuilt.

So Barak's family lived in a tent like everyone else in Ramah. There were a couple of differences though. First, as they worked every day, Deborah and Barak sang with their daughters. By now, the girls had learned many of the old songs of Israel as well as the songs Deborah and Barak had created themselves. The songs lifted their hearts and kept them from the despair of their neighbors.

The other thing they did have that few others in the town did was plenty of food since they hadn't lost any of their garden in Kedesh. In fact, they had an abundant supply of all sorts of fruits and vegetables as well as all the flour Deborah had ground from the last wheat harvest. So, Deborah and Mara kept a communal oven and cooking pot going all day long, and they gladly welcomed anyone who would come and eat freely.

At first, only a few of the men in the town would come, sending instead only the women and children, usually with a wooden bowl to take food home to *Abba*. But, by the end of the summer, there was a friendly rapport with everyone in town — with, of course, one exception. And by then, many of the other residents of Ramah had also taken up singing. Or whistling. Or playing on musical instruments. Often, the men would whistle as they did whatever work they could find to do, and it seemed they could always find something to do. Farmers became potters, or weavers, or carpenters, or shoe cobblers, or makers of musical instruments, or whatever. And as they sang and blessed *Adonai*, He began to again bless them.

A caravan of traders stopped by one morning, and when the traders saw all the fine things the townsmen had made, they bought nearly everything and promised they'd be back through at least twice a year to purchase whatever the men could give them if they were as fine in quality as these items.

"Push, Deborah, push." Deborah stood over the birthing stool with *Ima* Mara kneeling at her feet. "I can see the head."

"No, it's too early yet. He will be too small." Deborah fought the pains, but they were too strong, and she did as *Ima* Mara had commanded.

Mara shook her head. "I don't think so. Not from the size of this head."

When the pain was over, Deborah gasped for breath. "How can you tell that? The head isn't out yet."

"Trust me. I've been doing this a lot of years. I think you were right. It's a boy, and he's a big one."

Deborah laughed. "Oh, Mara, I've been telling you that for months, and you didn't believe me. Now, before he comes out, you're sure?"

She breathed deeply as another surge came.

"Here, bite down on this towel and push again as hard as you can."

"Whaaaah."

"The head's out! Strong cries. Hang on, don't push. I've got to make sure the cord is clear. That's good. One shoulder is out. One last push. That's it! It is a boy! We have a son! We have a son! Oh, Deborah, except for his father, he's the most beautiful boy I've ever seen! I've delivered a lot of babes. But he's the most perfect. Look, his skin isn't even that red." Swiftly she tied the cord and sliced it with the carving knife she'd run through the fire ahead of time.

"Here, put him to your breast. I still have work to do. If you can, push again. Once more. That's it. Now you can relax. Your work is done. You are no longer considered barren in the eyes of Israel, and I am no longer cursed."

"Oh, Mara," Deborah cried, "You were never cursed. Don't you know how much *Adonai* loves you?" She put her free arm around the older woman's shoulder.

Tears of joy came to Mara's eyes. "No, I don't suppose I do. After my other son died, Abinoam took to drink, and after a while we'd lost everything, I was sure I was cursed. And then all my grandchildren were girls, and I knew our name would die out, so I was even more certain of it. Barak is such a good son, and I have always felt blessed by having a sweet daughter-in-law and my beautiful granddaughters, no matter what others thought, but it's just nice to have others recognize that too. It makes me almost want to sing like you and Barak do. I just don't have the voice for it."

Smiling broadly, Deborah assured her, "That doesn't matter. All *Adonai* desires is a joyful noise. When we sing praise, it tells Him how much we love Him."

Mara whispered, "But if I sing, does that mean He will take away our son, like He took Ehud's house when Barak sang?"

Deborah shook her head vehemently. "Oh, of course not! I'd be more worried about what He might do if you didn't sing when He's obviously prompted you to."

"You're sure?" At Deborah's nod, she lifted her voice. "Okay, I'll do it. Don't say I didn't warn you about how badly I sing. 'Praise be to You, Oh *Adonai* our Lord, Maker of the world, Keeper of our faith, for Your blessings upon us, and for giving us this day a son to lift up Your name and spread forth Your praise.'"

Ima Mara was right. She didn't have a beautiful voice or the natural musicality of her son, Barak, but Deborah was blessed by the song. "Oh, *Ima* Mara, that was so beautiful. Not only did you praise *Adonai*, but you pronounced a blessing on our son. He now has a destiny to fulfill. And I think you have given him a name; it shall be Halal."

Mara beamed. She took the babe from Deborah's breast. "Why don't you get some rest now, while I tell my son it's time to plant a cedar tree! While that is being done, I will take Halal out to meet his sisters? We'll wrap him in his bindings, and we will let my son and Halal's sisters pronounce their own blessings on him." Tenderly she kissed the babe's forehead. "He's already a blessing, isn't he? Just like my Barak."

CHAPTER
13

And every male among you who is eight days old shall be circumcised throughout your generations. Genesis 17:12a

Deborah threw her arms around Barak. "Beloved, it is time. You must gather workers and hurry to pick the olives. The girls and *Ima* Mara can go with you, but you will need as many helpers as you can find."

"Shouldn't we wait until you can go with us? Halal will need to be circumcised before we can get back. And…"

"Shhh… It is arranged. *Ima* Mara has talked with the shoe cobbler. He has agreed to come and be the *mohel*. He will do the *brit milah* and say the blessing. The olives won't wait. Just be sure to instruct the older ones to take sticks and beat the branches hard yet carefully and let the younger ones gather all the olives that fall. They may not go back through and beat a second time, or pick to the edges of the grove. Those olives are for the poor. Go through Ramah and offer to pay every worker a *shekel* for their help and let each family receive an *ephah* of olives and an *omer* of oil for their own use. I think you'll be surprised how many will go with you."

As usual, Deborah was right. By the time Barak had been through Ramah, he had a small army of workers. Most of them had their own donkeys to carry back their own olives, so when they left town, they looked like a small caravan.

As he looked back on the town, he smiled. How much better it looked! Almost all of the houses had been repaired now, including Ehud's, and thanks to all that rain, once again the hillsides were teeming with a variety of trees and vegetation.

As they headed toward Jerusalem, he, *Ima* Mara, and the girls began to sing the song of Moses. Soon most of the townspeople had joined in, and their procession was more like a victory parade than a work detail.

"Please be gentle," Deborah begged. "Don't hurt him."

Seth, the old shoe cobbler, smiled an almost toothless grin at her and at Sair, the only other man in town who hadn't gone to pick olives. He would have probably refused to come, but couldn't find any acceptable excuse not to welcome Halal into the covenant of Abraham. "Don't worry. I have six sons and many grandsons. I have done this many times before. There isn't really any way for it not to hurt him, but I will make it as painless as possible."

He placed a piece of wine-soaked cloth into the babe's mouth for him to suck on. Seth ran his blade back and forth over the sharpening stone before he took Halal into his arm and said the blessing. *"Baruch atah Adonai Eloheinu Melech ha-olam, asher kidshanu b'mitzvotav v'tzivanu l'hakhniso bivrito shel Avraham avinu."*

Sair and Deborah both said "Amen."

Then Seth asked Deborah for the babe's name, repeated another blessing and loosened the foreskin before beginning. "The key is to have the knife as sharp as possible. That way it slides easily over the foreskin, and see there, it is done."

He gently cleaned the affected area and wiped the blood away before laying the babe back into his cradle. "He barely cries at all."

Of course even as he said that, Halal let out a lusty wail, and Deborah rushed to take him and soothe him.

"That cry has nothing to do with the pain. It's merely a demand for his *Ima*'s attention," Seth assured her.

"I know. But I needed to hold him nearly as much as he needed me to do it. Thank you for being our *mohel*, Seth. And Sair, as Halal's only male witness, I guess that makes you his *kwater*. I appreciate so much that you came to be here for him in the absence of his father. Thank you. There is food for both of you on the table in the courtyard. If you will excuse me, I'll take Halal to my room to see to his needs now."

For the first time, Sair spoke. "I am honored to do so, Deborah. Halal is blessed to have such a wise and generous mother and father. I have heard the songs of our people, and I know that many of our townspeople have hope today because of the wisdom of Barak and Deborah. You could have come back with hired workers and fixed Ehud's house in no time, but instead you lived in a tent when you didn't have to, shared your food with all who would come, and you taught us to sing again. For that we owe you a great debt of gratitude."

"Amen," Seth agreed.

The praise was the last thing Deborah had expected to hear coming from Sair. This must be why *Adonai* had refused to let her curse him. She stared at him for several moments. "So why didn't you go out to pick olives?"

He laughed. "My wives and children are with Barak. I'm far too old to pick olives." He tweaked Halal's toe. "Besides, I knew that you needed at least one more man here for the circumcision ceremony."

She hesitated again before speaking further. Perhaps it would be best to leave well enough alone. But she had to know. "So, does that mean you would no longer object if I judged in the city gate?"

He didn't speak for a time. "No, I won't object."

"Thank you, Sair. That's so wonderful to know. You don't know how much I appreciate it. But *Adonai* has shown me that I'm already right where He wants me to be. I don't need a city gate. My message is for all the people of Israel, not just for Ramah. There is great danger ahead for us."

"Yes. Things are getting more and more desperate. Every day I hear news of Jabin's conquests. So far, he's confined himself to isolated raids in the north, but he's getting bolder and closer."

Deborah nodded. "Yes, but that isn't the true problem. The real problem is that we have grown so much weaker. The people are forsaking the ways of *Adonai* and going after the *Baalim* and playing the harlot in the *Asherah* groves, and they are teaching their children to do the same or worse. I think that's one reason why I am called to sit among the palm trees. *Baal* and *Ashtoreth* are no match for *Adonai*. They must flee from His presence."

Sair nodded, and coughed. "Yes, well, you're certainly right about that. Nevertheless, I do apologize for my former stubbornness. I have heard word of many of your judgments, and I couldn't fault even one as being anything other than exactly what Ehud would have said under the circumstances. You will have no further trouble from me. I will daily pray for the continued blessing of *Adonai* on you and your household. One last thing. I know that Barak believes I had something to do with Ehud's house burning down, and I can't blame him after the way I behaved, but I swear to you, I didn't. I don't know who did it. If I did, I would help you to get justice against him."

"Well, we won't worry about that for today. The truth always comes to light sooner or later. You two go on out and eat and drink. Today is a day of celebration."

CHAPTER 14

When the days of her purification are completed,
for a son or for a daughter, she shall bring to the priest at the doorway of
the tent of meeting a one year old lamb for a burnt offering and a young
pigeon or a turtledove for a sin offering.
Leviticus 12:6

Barak brought Deborah up to the doorway of the Tabernacle where he had already brought Eli the priest out to meet her. Eli was a rather short and round man with thin hair and beard; certainly nothing much to look at. He wore a beautifully woven robe with a bejeweled ephod and golden bells and purple and scarlet pomegranates.

Although she had thought she knew exactly what it would look like, the glittering ornamentation of the garment was astonishingly beautiful, far more impressive than she had expected. *Adonai* certainly desired his priests to come into his presence in royal splendor.

"Eli, this is my wife, Deborah, and this is our son, Halal."

When Eli spoke, his voice was a bit high-pitched and slightly scratchy sounding, as if he had something caught in his throat. But his words were kind and gracious. "Blessed be the Name of *Adonai* for His graciousness in bringing us to this moment. It is so nice to finally meet the wonderful lady who has lit up *Adonai*'s tabernacle so beautifully. Before, it was so dim in there, I thought my eyes would give out before I had seen thirty summers. And I have heard such great things about the wisdom from *Adonai* you have shared with many who have come to you for judgment."

Deborah bowed her head low. "Thank you," she whispered. "May you be blessed also for your service here in this holy place. Later, my husband has some oil to show you that will make the lamps burn even brighter. But first, we have brought my purification offering, as well as a grain offering and the offering of our first fruits."

Eli rubbed his hands together with a smile. "That's wonderful. I'll send my son Phinehas out to help you bring everything in. He's still very young, but he's strong. Wait here while I go get him."

Only a few moments later, he returned with a young boy about the age of the twins, in a white tunic indicating his priestly lineage, but still allowing him the freedom to play like any other young boy his age. Something about him was like the spoiled young Jacob, although he moved quickly to follow his *Abba*'s command to help bring in the offerings. But when he jumped up onto the wagon and swiftly began to gobble up olives, Deborah frowned.

"Stop that right now, young man." Barak pulled the boy down off the wagon.

"Why?" The child tried to again climb up onto the wagon and get to the olives.

"Because those are a first-fruit offering." Barak restrained him.

"So what? The first-fruit offering belongs to the priests, and my *Abba* is the priest, so it's mine!" He yelled at Barak in a manner no child had a right to scream at a grown man, even if he was a priest's son.

Barak attempted to keep his voice down. "Not until it's been blessed and offered to *Adonai* as our first-fruit offering it isn't! Now stay down! Go back inside if you must, but you will stay away from our offering until it's been properly made!"

The little boy went running back into priest's quarters, crying for his *Ima.*

"Please forgive my son for his rash behavior," Eli murmured as Barak brought up the last of the proffered offerings. "He means well, but he is still too young to fully understand the ways of *Adonai.*"

"A few good spankings could solve that in a hurry," Barak growled.

Eli sighed. "I know, but his *Ima* doesn't believe that spankings are good for a child's sense of worth. She doesn't want me to spank him. I think it's because her own *Abba* beat her terribly. I have seen the scars, so I can understand why she feels the way she does."

"Unfortunately, men do seem to go to one extreme or the other." Deborah sighed. "Although, my Barak is the exception to that rule." She patted his arm. "He seems to have found the perfect balance. Our girls so love their *Abba*, but he doesn't let them get away with any misbehavior at all. I only hope the same will hold true with our son. I'm told boys are harder to discipline than girls are. But abuse is not discipline, nor discipline abuse. Children need the one, but certainly not the other."

Eli nodded. "That's so true, and I do try. But so far, it doesn't seem to be working. My two sons are so young, but so strong willed. I will admit I just don't seem to have the strength to change them."

Barak took his hand. "For the sake of Israel, you must find the strength, my friend. Your sons are the future priests of Israel. We need them to be strong men of *Adonai.*"

If she hadn't just been thinking about him such a short time ago, Deborah might not have recognized Jacob when she saw him right outside the city gate. He was jumping around, excitedly bartering with a trader. As she gazed at him to make sure she wasn't mistaken in her identification, he happened to glance up, and obviously recognized her too. He took off running.

She grabbed Barak's arm. "Stop him! Quickly! Don't let him get away!"

"What? Who?"

Deborah pointed at the figure running away from them. Barak flicked the reins and headed the donkey toward him. But, of course, the donkey took that moment to show why donkeys have such a reputation for stubbornness. Barak jumped down off the cart and took off after the young man. He wouldn't have had any chance of actually catching him, but at least his chase caught the attention of some of the other men of Shiloh, and soon Jacob was in the clutches of several men.

"Is he a thief?"

"What did he steal from you?"

"Who is he? Is this your son?"

When Barak finally caught his breath, he shrugged. "I don't know. Ask my wife. She's the one who recognized him."

Somehow, Deborah had managed to get the donkey to come their way. She jumped off the cart. "Yes, he's a thief," Deborah put her hands on her hips. "He has stolen a bride from her lawful husband. Where is Chesed, Jacob? What have you done with her?"

"I am not a thief. Joshua was the one who stole her from me! I'm the one who was wronged. Chesed is my bride. She always was, and now she always will be."

"Where is she?" Barak grabbed the boy from the men, and held him up off the ground by his silken cloak.

"Where you'll never find her," he snarled. "And if you don't put me down immediately, and I don't get back to her, she's going to starve to death. Is that what you all want? You take me, and you kill her!" When Barak slowly put him down, he defiantly crossed his arms and stared back at them all with a self-satisfied smirk.

Deborah restrained Barak from putting his fist right into that smirk.

"Has anyone seen his wagon?" Barak looked around. "Do any of you know where it is?"

The trader stepped up. "He didn't bring a wagon this time. He came on a camel. That's it right over there. But I've seen him here before with a girl. She stayed up on the camel though. I think she's pregnant!"

CHAPTER
15

If a man has committed a sin worthy of death and he is put to death, and you hang him on a tree, his corpse shall not hang all night on the tree, but you shall surely bury him on the same day (for he who is hanged is accursed of God).
Deuteronomy 21:22-23a

Under the circumstances, Deborah and Barak stayed in Shiloh, at least for the time being. They found a room at a local inn, and daily Deborah tried to convince Jacob to tell them where he had left Chesed. The search for her went on for days, but the problem was that a camel could travel long distances even in rough wilderness terrain. Without knowing which direction to go, how could they possibly find a lone girl?

Barak had immediately sent a messenger to Kedesh to go to both Jacob's and Chesed's parents. But what could they do either? And even if they did find her, would they be bringing her back only to be stoned for infidelity?

Even though he claimed to love her, Jacob adamantly refused to tell them where to find Chesed. If he was going to die, so was she, he declared.

When the messenger returned, he brought not only Chesed and Jacob's parents, but Joshua and his *Abba* and *Ima* too.

Immediately, Joshua asked for permission to talk with Jacob. Since neither Deborah nor anyone else had been able to get through to the boy, what could it hurt? "But Joshua, if you hurt Jacob, you could be punished too. I don't want that to happen, and neither would Chesed. So, why else would you want to talk with Jacob?"

"I won't hurt him. I promise. I just want him to tell me where to find Chesed. She needs me. I can help her."

"You heard the man say that she's carrying Jacob's baby, didn't you? And Jacob seemed to confirm that. He said she was his wife now, and always would be, and nothing could change that."

Tears ran down Joshua's face. "I know. But it's not her fault. He forced her. I saw the blood on her headscarf. She fought him. He took her. It's not her fault. "

"So, does that mean you would still have her as your wife? Even with another man's baby?"

Slowly, he nodded. "I've already talked it over with *Ima* and *Abba*. Chesed is the kindest girl I've ever met. All the other girls laughed at me because I was so big and clumsy and hairy, and I'm not nearly as smart or talented as most of the boys my age were. But not Chesed! She said I was going to be a good man, and that I could do whatever I had a mind to do! Well, I have a mind to save my wife!"

"In that case, you just might. Come on, let's go talk to Jacob. Maybe if you told him that, it might persuade him to let Chesed live."

But Jacob seemed to take an evil delight in tormenting Joshua this one last time. Jacob was to hang first thing in the morning, but he would face *Adonai*'s judgment and take his secret to his grave.

CHAPTER 16

Hear a just cause, O Lord, give heed to my cry;
Give ear to my prayer, which is not from deceitful lips. Psalm 17:1

The next day, after the hanging of Jacob, both David and Joshua's family were ready to head back to Kedesh, although Micah and his family would remain in Shiloh for at least a week for the burial and mourning of his son.

But with Halal safely strapped onto her back, and Barak leading the way, Deborah finally caught up with them right before they reached the city gate to leave. "No," she cried breathlessly, "please don't go yet. Last night I fervently prayed, and I have had a vision from *Adonai*. Chesed is not yet dead, and we can't let Jacob win this. But he will if we can't find her soon."

"But how?" David looked down from his perch aboard his camel. "Men have already been out searching for days. Where else would we look? And tomorrow is *Shabbat*, so we won't have much time."

Deborah took his outstretched hand. "I don't think she's that far from here. I don't think he trusted Chesed enough to travel further than he could go and get back in one day."

He seemed to consider that and bent the camel down to talk further. "But then why wouldn't she have come to town by now? When he didn't return, why didn't she run for her life? For that matter, why didn't she take off the moment he left her alone?"

Halal began to cry, and Deborah pulled her sling around to rock him and gently soothe him back to sleep. "Maybe she's too afraid," she whispered. "If she is with child, surely Jacob would have convinced her by now that she is as guilty as he is, and that if he is caught, she would be stoned right along with him. He could have filled her mind with all kinds of fears and lies to make her bend to his will."

"Let's go with her, please *Abba*," Joshua begged from their donkey cart. "I believe her. I feel it in my bones that Chesed lives. We must help her."

The older man, Obediah, nodded fiercely. "I agree with my son." He waved his hand to Deborah. "Lead the way!"

She laughed. "Actually, my thought was to let Micah's camel lead the way."

David descended from his own camel and laughingly rubbed its nose. The camel affectionately returned his gesture by licking his face. "Don't you know that camels are the dumbest, most stubborn creatures ever born? They make donkeys seem docile by comparison. What makes you think that beast could find my daughter?"

"No, I don't know any such thing." Deborah shook her head. "Personally, I've always found camels to be pretty smart. Especially when you treat them nicely and sing to them, they walk faster and in a straight line. My *Saba* had a camel named Anna, and she was the gentlest, smartest animal I ever met. I suppose camels are a lot like people. There are smart ones, and dumb ones, and a lot somewhere in between. Let's hope Micah has a smart one. But let's hope even more that *Adonai* takes control of the animal and, whether he's smart or dumb, it really makes no difference because he's being led by the Spirit of *Adonai*. That's my prayer."

"Amen," said Joshua and his *Abba* in chorus.

"Amen," David agreed. "Let's go get that camel."

Of course, that meant they had to let Micah in on their plan. In his present state of grief, he wasn't at all convinced that it would do any good, but finally agreed to let them have the camel if there was any chance at all of bringing Chesed back alive and at least lifting the sin of murder from his son's wickedness. David offered to leave him his own camel in exchange, but Micah said that wasn't necessary. He wasn't going anywhere to need a camel anyway.

At first, it seemed that David was right. This was a very dumb and stubborn camel indeed, but as Deborah soothingly sang to her and let her have her head, she finally began to walk straight toward the mountain. "That's a girl," Deborah whispered into her ear. "Show us where Chesed is. You can do it, girl."

After a while, Halal began to cry. Deborah would have to tend to his needs. But she didn't want the camel to stop walking. "Beloved, could you please come up here a moment," she called out. When Barak arrived, she whispered, "I need to feed and change Halal. Please sing with me until the camel gets used to your voice. Then I will leave you to sing to her alone. It keeps her calm. Don't try to guide her. Just let her walk where she wishes."

So they sang together, and David, Obediah, and Joshua joined in. Oddly, the camel too began to bray as if she also was giving praise to *Adonai*. Maybe she wasn't as dumb as Deborah had thought.

After she had tended to Halal's needs, Deborah rejoined Barak at the front. They were nearing the mountain. The camel began to bray louder and veer off to the left. Deborah bit her lip. Until she spotted a path—and camel prints! She kissed the camel's cheek "You did it girl! Look everyone! Camel prints coming down the mountain. Let's hurry! Sing louder!"

It did seem that the louder they sang, the faster the animals climbed. Even the donkey kept up with the longer-legged camels. Of course, that may have been because Joshua was pushing him to his utmost limits, but he didn't seem to mind. It was as if the Spirit of *Adonai* was pushing him along too. Joshua hurried ahead, and Deborah rushed to keep up with him, leaving the others a ways behind. Suddenly they were at a cave.

"Chesed," Deborah called. No answer. "Chesed, are you in there?" Still no answer.

"Beloved," Joshua called, his deep voice almost echoing into the darkness. "If you're here, please don't be afraid. We're here to rescue you, not to harm you. I love you, and I still want you to be my wife. No one will hurt you. I promise."

"Joshua, is it truly you, my beloved?" a voice cried weakly. "Please help me! I can't get out!"

"It's her!" Joshua called to everyone, but again not waiting for anyone, he took off running into the depths of the cave. Darkness swallowed him up.

"Someone get the lamps," Deborah called. "And bring some water and blankets and the bandages! I have a feeling we're going to need them!"

CHAPTER 17

The Lord also will be a stronghold for the oppressed, A stronghold in times of trouble. Psalm 9:9

Despite his claims, Jacob had never been able to break Chesed's spirit. Yes, he had broken quite a few bones. And yes, she was pregnant. But she wasn't his wife. She was his prisoner, a prisoner barely able to walk, much less run, half-starved, and out of water, but kept in the dark recess of the cave only by a huge stone it took all the men to roll away. Still, the stone wasn't quite large enough to seal the recess, and she had dug around it and managed to make a hole large enough to get her hand through to keep digging. How in the world had Jacob gotten it into place?

This must be meant to be a burial cave. Rolling it in was downhill. That was the easy part. Deborah shuddered. Jacob had never intended to come back. He had intended for Chesed to die in this place. And the child to die with her. That's what he had meant when he said she would be his wife forever.

After they had gotten Chesed to drink a little wine mixed with hyssop, eat a tiny bit of the lentil soup Deborah had brought, and

Deborah had set and bandaged her broken bones, Chesed seemed to feel the need to talk, to explain to Joshua that she had never wanted any of this. She admitted that Jacob had raped her repeatedly. Tearfully, she told them all that she had cried out, but that he had both a knife and a club, and that he had used the club to break her leg so she couldn't run away.

"Even then, I swear, I tried to fight him off, but it only seemed to excite him more. See the scars!" She pulled aside the robe so they could see. "After a while, I stopped fighting. What good did it do? He said I was his wife now, and a man could do anything he wanted to his wife. He believed that too. That's why I never wanted to marry him in the first place. I knew how cruel he could be." She put her hand to her abdomen. "Even as a boy, he loved to pull the wings off of butterflies and mutilate voles and squirrels when no one was around to stop him. I saw him do it, and it made me sick to my stomach. Will his child be like that?"

Deborah shook her head. "Not necessarily. Not if you teach him or her the virtues of kindness and love. Can you do that?"

Chesed shrugged. "I don't know. What if every time I look at the baby I remember all of this?"

Deborah put an arm around her. "That may happen for a while. It may even happen for a long time. But you have to remember it's not the baby's fault. Babies come into the world sweet and innocent. Usually they learn good or evil from the people around them. I know you're good. And I know Joshua is good. I think with the right guidance from you both, this baby can be good too. You just have to have the strength and the wisdom to rely on *Adonai* to make it happen. Maybe it would be best if your family could move to a new place where you can all get a fresh start without everyone knowing the circumstances of your baby's birth."

Chesed agreed to think about it.

"Why didn't you tell your *Abba* why you didn't want to marry Jacob?"

"Because my *Abba* loved Jacob's *Abba* like a brother, and truly, Jacob's *Abba* is one of the kindest men I've ever met. You said babies learn evil from those around them, but truly, I don't know where Jacob got his cruel nature. His *Ima* was always very kind to me. At least, she was until she found out I wasn't going to marry Jacob. Then she was angry, but I don't really blame her for that. She loves Jacob a lot, and she didn't understand why I would hurt him. I didn't want to hurt either of them."

"But why didn't you ask for help when you were in Shiloh?" Joshua asked in his soft voice. "That's what I don't understand. They said you never said a word."

She lowered her eyes ashamedly. "Because Jacob said if I did, he'd not only kill me, but he'd kill whoever I told, too." She took Deborah's hands. "He would have done it too. He had a short dagger hidden in the sleeve of his cloak the whole time we were there. I know he would have used it if I'd told. Why was he like that?"

Deborah shook her head. It was one of those questions she had asked herself many times over the years as she had watched Ehud judge. This was the first time she'd seen it to such an extent in one of her own cases though. "I don't know. It seems that *HaSatan* just gets into some people and turns them evil."

"But what will happen to me now? Even if I got rid of the baby, I am disgraced in the eyes of the people. I can't go home."

"Not all people," Deborah declared. "It seems to me you're very blessed. You have a man who loves you so much that he's willing to take you and your child to be his own family. And your family and his family will be there for you to see you through this whole thing. My family will be there for you too, if you want or need anything."

Chesed wrapped the blanket tighter around herself. "Then I'm truly not going to be stoned or hanged?"

Deborah patted her hand. "No, you're not. Why would you be? Everyone here can testify that you had no choice. Jacob is already dead. He was hanged this morning. He can't hurt you anymore. I promise."

CHAPTER 18

Now the sons of Eli were worthless men; they did not know the Lord. 1 Samuel 2:12

Eli never did find the strength to discipline his sons. It seemed that every time Deborah saw them, Phinehas and Hophni had grown more rebellious and evil. She was prejudiced because she was his mother, but Halal seemed to have the sweetest nature she had ever seen in a child.

Halal was nearly four now, and almost never seemed to need the discipline the girls had needed. Sometimes it rather worried Deborah that he was so gentle and compliant. Weren't little boys supposed to be rebellious and boisterous? True to his name, he loved to sing with the sweetest little voice. Already he knew most of the songs of Israel better than Tamar did. Living up to his name even further, he was always going about making his own little praise songs. She loved to hear his sweet little-boy voice singing his favorite:

In good times, Halal sing [Hal]lelujah.
In bad times, Halal sing [Hal]lelujah
In good, in bad, [Hal]lelujah, Halal, [Hal]lelujah, [Hal]lelujah!

Of course, he wasn't quite old enough yet to form the [Hal] sound properly, so it would come out "Alal" and "lalelujah, lalelujah, lalelujah!"

After a while, even the girls were singing it the same way, and Deborah had to laughingly scold them that he would never learn to sing it correctly if they didn't teach him the right way to say the words.

It did allay her fears about his gentle nature somewhat that he was curious and intelligent, asking many questions about everything he observed. He did tend to observe everything, even the things she wouldn't think would interest a young boy at all.

"Why is the sky so red like that? Why do voles only come out at night?" But it was a sweet curiosity and a kind nature that brought joy and laughter to the lips of all he encountered.

Still, all the questions could sometimes be hard. "Why do *Abba* and I sleep in one room and you and *Safta* Mara and my sisters sleep in the other? Why? …why? …why?"

Never had she seen such a curious child. And sometimes she didn't really want to take the time to answer.

Today was one of those days. Barak had returned from Shiloh with a lamb. It was *Abib*, and almost time for *Pesach*. Phineas had claimed the lamb Barak had taken to Shiloh for blessing had some kind of imaginary blemish, and insisted he buy a new one. Of course, he had also wanted Barak to leave the old one as part of the price of the new one. He intended to sell it to the next man as part of his evil scheme.

Barak was in a foul mood, and it had done nothing to help Deborah's own mood. She and the girls had been cleaning the house furiously all day while he was gone, and she shooed him out the door to go to talk with some of his friends about the wickedness of the young priests.

Tamar was given the honor of finding the last bit of *hametz* and taking it outside to burn it. Next year, after his weaning ceremony, it would be Halal's turn to burn the *hametz*. Already he wanted to "help." He ran after Tamar, chattering incessantly as always, asking what was *hametz*? Why did they have to take it outside? Why did they burn it? What was sin?

Poor little Tamar was so busy trying to answer his questions, she never saw the magnificent black stallion pulling the iron-clad chariot with its huge iron scythes on the wheels as it bore down on them. But Deborah saw it, and so did Rachel and Jael. Deborah screamed, but she was inside the house looking out through the window, and couldn't get outside in time. Rachel was the one who ran out into the street, and, with all her strength, threw her brother and sister to safety only moments before she was crushed by the giant horse's hooves and pierced by the scythe of the iron-clad wheels.

The driver of the chariot never stopped or looked back.

CHAPTER
19

For I will go through the land of Egypt on that night, and will strike down all the firstborn in the land of Egypt, both man and beast; and against all the gods of Egypt I will execute judgments − I am the Lord.
Exodus 12:12

The next several days were a blur to Deborah. It was *Pesach*, and *Adonai*'s angel of death had taken her firstborn. Why? What had she done wrong? Were the men of Ephraim right? Was she being punished for the sin of pride? She didn't speak through Barak like Ehud had told her to. Was that the problem? Had the little bee become enamored of her own voice? She didn't think so. She had always tried to give all the glory to *Adonai*, but maybe she had somewhere hidden in her a speck of leaven.

But what had Rachel done wrong? Yes, she had coveted Jael's comb, but that was back when she was a child, not yet considered accountable under the law. Hadn't she more than made up for it since then? Didn't saving her brother and sister prove that she was worthy to live?

The questions swirled in Deborah's head, and wouldn't go away. Somehow, Rachel must have been buried. Somehow, a *Pesach* meal must have been served, and she must have been a part of it, but she couldn't have told anyone about any of it. The winter was over and spring had come, but Deborah had never felt so cold in her life. Even nursing Halal was too much for her. Her paps refused to give any milk, and Halal had to be weaned early. If they had held a weaning ceremony, Deborah didn't remember it.

The house still had four children in it. Four children who especially needed their *Ima* right now, but Deborah couldn't seem to make herself move. It was as if the voices all around her had no sound, and couldn't reach into her being. Even Barak couldn't break through the wall of silence she had built. He was hurting, too. She knew that. She should want to help him. She should want to help her children. How could she? She couldn't help herself.

And yet, Barak later told her that she had moved and talked and behaved exactly as she always had during those days. He said she had taken charge of the burial and the preparations for the *Pesach* meal herself. He said she had kissed and comforted the children, and washed and wrapped the body and even fed the mourners. Other than that she couldn't nurse, they had worried that she wasn't grieving enough.

Deborah wasn't sure exactly when she began to come back to life. The seven weeks of counting the *omer* and saying the appropriate blessing for each day were almost over before she realized that she had continued to live. Soon it would be *Shavuot*, the festival of the first fruits, the giving of thanks for Moses receiving the law on Mt. Sinai. And she was thankful. She did want to live again. When had that happened?

Maybe it was at the *chalaka*, Halal's first haircut, when she had cried almost as pathetically as he had that they were taking away his beautiful curls; or maybe it was the night of the bonfire and dancing when Barak had kissed her and they had returned home, hand-in-hand, to come together again for the first time, or maybe it was simply the first time she had again lifted her voice to join Halal in his little song of praise that she didn't really feel like singing with him, but had done it anyway.

It almost seemed wrong that she could go on. Parents weren't supposed to outlive their children. Young girls who hadn't yet tasted the sweetness of life shouldn't be taken from it. Oh, that *Adonai* had deemed it better to take her and spare her daughter. She was old, and probably past the age of bearing any more children. How many generations of children were lost in the taking of Rachel? In one more year, she would have been married. Barak had already had inquiries about her *mohar,* and a suitable betrothal was already in the works. Now who would the young man marry?

All she could do was pray, "*Baruch atah Adonai, Dayan ha-emet.* Blessed are You, *Adonai*, the true Judge."

CHAPTER 20

*Vengeance is Mine, and retribution, in due time their foot will slip;
For the day of their calamity is near, and the impending things are
hastening upon them. Deuteronomy 32:35*

Barak's grief was no less real, but it expressed itself in a different way. He was angry, and he was determined to find the man who had run down his little girl, and make him pay! He went through the town talking to everyone, whether man, woman, or child, trying to find out if anyone knew who the charioteer was. Several people had seen the chariot speed through town, but descriptions of the man in the chariot varied.

Some swore it was one of Sisera's aides. A few swore that it was the great commander himself. But, when asked if they had ever actually seen Sisera, all admitted they had not. All they had was the rumor that Sisera was a giant of a man with long hair and a long beard and a voice that could fell trees with its resonance. Everyone was agreed that it was a large black stallion leading the chariot, and Sisera was known for his magnificent black stallion, but surely he wasn't the only one in his army with a black horse.

Nevertheless, whether it was him or one of his men, as far as Barak was concerned Sisera was responsible. When children couldn't even play in the streets of their own town, something had to be done. Sisera had an army. It was time Israel had an army too!

Sair was the first in town to agree with Barak. He had nowhere near the wealth he used to, but he had recovered a good bit of what he had lost, and what he did have, he pledged to Barak in aid of the cause. But he said they weren't anywhere near ready to fight Sisera yet. They needed to recruit and build an army, to learn to fight like Sisera's army fought, and to find the perfect times and places to strike. Sisera and his army didn't just go in and mow down an entire country, Sair declared. They were selective in their strikes, and they struck when it was least expected. But with *Adonai* on their side, surely they could learn to outfox the foxes.

Barak had to agree with Sair's logic, but waiting was hard. Sair had said the first step was to recruit an army, so everywhere he went, though he ostensibly went to sell torches and oil, his primary purpose was to make friends to support the cause and to convince as many men of fighting age of the need to fight against Sisera. As Sisera's raids continued, and more and more people were killed or maimed, or wives or daughters were raped and mutilated, that task became easier and easier.

For the protection of Deborah and his children, he needed to find a way to keep his efforts separate. 'Lappidoth the Torchman' became the seller of wicks and olive oil, while 'Barak the General' organized an army for Israel. Only a few ever knew they were one and the same. For a good while, even Deborah didn't know what he was up to.

Maybe that was because he sold just as many wicks and just as much oil as he ever had; maybe even a little more. Maybe it was because his passion for justice carried over into his entire being, and he had an exuberance for life that he hadn't felt in a long time.

But maybe it was also because now he did see himself as fulfilling Ehud's prophecy and following in the footsteps of the

Joshua of old when he marched around Jericho and sent the walls tumbling. He intended to see them tumble right onto Sisera's head! Deborah had told him he would soon be too busy to play nursemaid to her. This had to be what she meant. This was his destiny!

And speaking of Joshua... Barak slapped his knee as he thought about his own gentle young giant. Who knew the boy could become such an excellent captain? Joshua had almost single-handedly recruited every fighting-aged man in Bethel. And they were much further ahead in their training than any of Barak's other squads. Joshua's wealthy father-in-law had funded their operation, and they were rapidly building a stockpile of weapons by forging swords and shields, making bows and arrows, and even gathering stones and making slingshots to carry on their belts in case all else failed. Deborah would be so proud of him if she knew.

CHAPTER
21

In the days of Shamgar the son of Anath, in the days of Jael, the highways
were deserted, and travelers went by roundabout ways. Judges 5:6

It was almost *Pesach* again. Soon it would be a year since Rachel
had died. The period of mourning was over. People expected her to
go on; to forget. But sometimes the pain seemed sharper now than
it had before. Like when young Heber had come just last week,
mounted on his white horse, to claim Jael as his bride. He had taken
her back to his tent, which was pitched near the terebinth tree at
Zaanannim, near Kedesh. The whole town followed them back for
the wedding feast, a week-long event of feasting, dancing, and
celebration.

Deborah was truly glad for Jael and for her mother, Shachar,
whose own husband had died last year, shortly after the marriage
was arranged. Heber was a kind man, well-mannered, and as
hospitable as any Hebrew groom would have been. The week of
feasting on fatted calves, flowing wine, figs, dates, honey cakes, and
pomegranates was even more sumptuous than the wealthiest

families of Ephraim would have been able to provide, especially in these hard times.

Jael did look glorious reclining on her wedding couch, with the twins as her honored attendants. Deborah loved Jael like one of her own daughters, and she felt guilty for wishing it was Rachel's wedding she was attending. Rachel would have been so beautiful being carried on that wedding couch with daisies threaded through her hair, and bells gently tinkling as she went by. Deborah would have made her a new festal robe for her wedding—a wedding that would now never be.

Halal shook her hand. "*Ima, Ima,* come and dance. Isn't Jael a most beautiful bride? Will I have a bride like Jael someday?"

She rubbed his head playfully. "Yes, my son. I'm sure you will."

But honestly, how could she be sure her young son would grow up and have a beautiful bride when Sisera's men could speed through a town on an iron chariot and crush a life with no more thought than she would have at swatting a gnat on her goat cheese?

When it was time for everyone to go home, the townspeople traveled as a group, like they had done to come to the feast. It wasn't safe to go any other way. They also took the back roads instead of the straight path, and walked in family groups with at least one man in each group. The highways were deserted these days. Most of the people who had lived in small outlying villages had now moved into the walled and fortified cities like Ramah, Bethel, and Kedesh.

Normally, they would have let all the men travel up front, with the women and children further behind them, but they didn't dare. Sisera's troops were always on the lookout for stray travelers to beat and rob of their provisions, and if they could separate the men from their wives, that was even better. Even stopping for water was a great danger. Wells were the perfect spot for thieves or a couple of Sisera's men to hide.

They were on them in moments, only four armed men on horseback against almost two dozen townspeople, but they were mostly women, and children. The soldiers had been waiting for them to come around the bend, with their swords and shields ready. Surprisingly, the men of Ramah were also ready. Some of the men stayed further back, out of range of the swords, throwing rocks as hard and as fast as they could throw them, aiming at the soldiers' heads so they would have to keep their shields up and couldn't see well enough to use their swords wisely.

Two other men climbed up onto the branch of the tree that had blocked their vision and swung down, knocking two of them off their horses and flat onto the road. When they did, Barak ran them through with a sword Deborah hadn't even known he carried. Then he dispatched the third soldier. Sair too had a sword, and he was fighting frantically to protect his family from the last soldier. He was losing the battle, but he needn't have worried. The two tree climbers had taken the swords from the felled soldiers and joined the fray. It was soon over and all four of Sisera's men were dead. Only the two townsmen who had been right at the front of their group had been badly injured, but Deborah was able to bandage them up and she was certain they would live.

"How did you do that?" Deborah gasped, as she bandaged a minor cut on Barak's arm.

He shrugged. "We've been practicing for months now. We talked about it on the way to the wedding, and we knew this might be a good place for an ambush, because coming from this direction you wouldn't see your attackers until you were right up on them. It's exactly the kind of place Sisera's men have been using to attack, although they haven't usually been quite this far south. That one chariot coming through Ramah was the only time I'd heard of his men being in Ephraim before now."

"But where did you get that sword? You've never had a sword before, and I didn't see you bring it."

"I took it off of another of Sisera's men when I killed him a few weeks back," Barak confessed. "Up near Kedesh. While I was off on my oil-selling trips. I've engaged his men a couple of times now with my troops, if you can call us that. We're really a bunch of farmers, carpenters and tradesmen who haven't yet quite learned how to properly wield a sword. But we are learning. You should see Joshua's squad from Bethel. They're the best we have. Are you angry with me for keeping this hidden from you?"

"No, why would I be?" She pointed at the dead soldiers. "Those men were here to kill all of us, and for what? We have almost no provisions, no horses, no jewels or anything valuable at all. What could they gain but the perverse pleasure of killing men and raping women and girls? I'm glad you're learning to fight back. How big is your army?"

"Only a few hundred men so far," he admitted. "And we're certainly no match for his iron chariots. But we're trying to learn from his own tactics and isolate and take out a few men at a time. Unfortunately, Sisera is starting to notice, and his men aren't quite as isolated as before. There were four of them this time instead of two. Before long, it'll be eight, then sixteen. He knows he has us outmanned by ten to one."

"Don't worry about that," she assured him. "One plus *Adonai* will always be enough."

Barak called his men to search the bodies and take anything that might be useful. He also commanded a man to take the horses to their mountain hiding place, and others to bury the soldiers' bodies before any more of Sisera's troops came raining down on them.

CHAPTER 22

You shall not set up for yourself a sacred pillar which the Lord your God hates. Deuteronomy 16:22

It hadn't been easy for Deborah to go back out to her judgment chair under the palm tree. *HaSatan* had tried to convince her that if she did she might lose another of her children, or something terrible might happen to Barak. After she found out what Barak had been up to for all those months, HaSatan's voice had started up again, and was even stronger. But, at the same time, Barak's activities convinced her all the more that Ehud had spoken the truth of *Adonai*'s plan. Barak was becoming the man of light that her country needed in these dark times.

And the times were getting so much darker. It seemed that *Asherah* poles had sprung up everywhere. At night, she could see shadowy figures in the palm groves up on the mountaintops, dancing in the moonlight. The *Baal* and *Ashtoreth* followers were becoming more blatant in their immoral practices, building their so-called 'temples' with prostitutes as 'priestesses' right here in *Adonai*'s nation, and doing lewd and despicable things in the name of 'worship.' She had even heard stories of women sacrificing their own babies to a god named *Molech* by passing them through a fire in a torturous death. How they could do such a thing to their own child was beyond her scope of understanding. She would gladly have given her own life to have her child back. They supposedly did all their wickedness for the sake of ears of corn and sheaves of barley.

But the more the evil spread, the less corn and barley there was. And less wheat and rye and figs and pomegranates. *Adonai* was angry, and Deborah couldn't blame Him. He Who had brought them out of the land of Egypt and fed them on manna and quail was being forsaken for wooden carvings of large-hipped women with no modesty. Did the people really believe these pieces of wood could help them, or were they simply an excuse to act out their frustration and indulge their own perverse desires? She didn't know, and truthfully, didn't care to find out. She wanted to help those who were seeking *Adonai*'s justice and mercy.

There were still many of those. Day after day, they would come, begging for her help. So she had gone back. Every day, she would pack up Halal and head for her palm tree.

After the twins had married two of Barak's cousins from Kedesh and been taken to their new homes, Tamar had taken on the duty of helping her *Safta* Mara with the cooking and housekeeping. Besides Halal, Joshua and Chesed had brought their son Eliab, and Sair had sent two of his grandsons to be instructed in the law by Deborah. She would spend mornings teaching the boys to read and write the laws of Moses on clay tablets. In the afternoons, they would listen to her hear cases and make rulings, and after everyone had gone, they could ask Deborah questions about why she had ruled the way she had. This was the way *Saba* Ehud had taught her.

Lately, a few older students of the law had also joined them and sometimes engaged Deborah in debate over her rulings. She didn't mind. Others of the town would also come out just to listen to the cases. Some were old women who had nothing better to do; a few just seemed to find it interesting and entertaining, and she was sure that there were some looking to find fault. Ehud had always said that it was good for a judge to be under constant scrutiny. It kept them honest and it kept them humble.

This day, Deborah was still teaching the boys when several men from Bethel came charging up the hill toward her, half carrying, half dragging a small, scantily-clad young woman with a badly bruised cheek and long dirt-caked black hair. The watchers parted, and the men dropped her at Deborah's feet.

Deborah stood, gathering her own robes around her. "What are your names, and why have you brought this woman here? Give her a robe. I have a young son and other young boys here. They don't need to be looking on her in that condition."

One of the men reluctantly took off his outer garment and gave it to the woman. "I'm Joram, son of Isa of the tribe of Benjamin, and the harlot here is Abigail. I brought her here because she was caught in the act of adultery, and I'm told you're a righteous judge of the law. I want her stoned immediately like the law demands."

Deborah's eyebrow arched. "Where is the man who was caught with her?"

The man who called himself Joram was taller and leaner, and perhaps slightly older, than most of his companions. He spoke harshly and with a mocking jeer. "Why does that matter? She was caught. My brother and I both saw her. We are both here to testify against her. You have your two witnesses. I want justice carried out now!"

"And you know for certain she is married?"

The man sneered again. "Yes, I do know she's married. She's married to my *Abba*."

Deborah stared at the two men. They themselves looked to be at least twice the woman's age. She couldn't have been much older than her Rachel would have been, had she lived. "So, I ask again. Where is the man? It takes two people to commit adultery, and both are equally liable under the law."

The tunic-clad man's brother whispered in his ear, and the first man rubbed his chin a bit before he finally answered. "He escaped out the back of the house through the courtyard."

Deborah walked toward the two of them, keeping her eyes directly on theirs. "But surely, if you both saw him in bed with your step-mother, you can identify him. You certainly have enough men with you to have apprehended him without difficulty. So, I ask you again. Why didn't you bring him here with you to face this?"

The way he stomped reminded her of Tamar when she was younger, having one of her famous temper tantrums. "Because he's not important, I tell you! She is. She must be stoned. It's the law!"

Deborah was becoming angry at the indifference to justice displayed by the supposed advocates for it. She went back to her chair to try to calm herself down before she spoke. "And it's also the law that he be stoned right along with her. He may not be important to you, but he is important to this court. Identify him now!"

They conferred again. Finally they spoke. "We'd rather not. He's a wealthy man of Bethel. It could cause severe trouble for us if we told."

Deborah shook her head. "If she is to be stoned, then he must be stoned also. The law does not allow for partial judgments, especially those favoring the wealthy over the poor, or those whose favor we seek over those we wish to be rid of. The law says if a man is found lying with a married woman, then both of them shall die. Why would you protect the man who lay with your father's wife? That doesn't make any sense to me at all. Besides, that woman has a badly bruised cheek. How do I know he didn't force himself on her? How do I know there even is a man? If there was, either you truly caught them in the act, in which case you're hiding something from me, or if he was escaping out the back when you entered as you say, you didn't actually see anything you could testify to at all, in which case you've lied to the court. Bring the man or release this woman immediately!"

The two huddled together again to talk. This time, all the friends with them got in on the discussion. Finally the tunic-clad one, who called himself Joram and looked to be the elder, spoke. "We can't bring the man. It would ruin our own business, and his family might take revenge. But we won't have that woman back in our home either. It would give our own wives and daughters the idea that there is no law in Israel and they could do as they pleased. If you won't have her stoned, we would have her divorced from our father."

Again Deborah brows raised. Unfortunately, divorce was easy enough for a man to obtain, but it was generally not a man's children who demanded it for him.

"Is your father here with you?" No one in the group of men looked nearly old enough to be their father. This was more like a rowdy bunch of ruffians who had been looking for trouble. The wonder was that they hadn't just stoned her themselves. Ah! That was it. Their intention had been a double blow. Knowing her to be a strict keeper of the law, they had thought to use this as a means to demean Deborah in the eyes of the women of Bethel as well as to get rid of the young woman who was somehow a threat to them.

"No, of course not. My father is old and feeble." Joram snapped.

"But not too feeble to take a young wife?"

"No. Evidently not," he agreed. "Old men are sometimes fools. Look what that foolishness brought him."

Something in his smug attitude didn't sit right. There was more to the story. "My question is, what did it bring you? Why do you hate your father's wife so much?"

For the first time during all of this time, the woman attempted to stand. As if she had suddenly awakened from a stupor, she pulled herself up to her full, if small, height and glared up at her accusers. "Because my husband was going to disinherit both of these two in favor of our son. I didn't know myself what was going on until just now when you asked that question. I thought they had truly come in and believed me guilty, but if I am found guilty of adultery, then maybe my husband would believe that our son is not his son, and they would again be his heirs."

Deborah gently took her hand and led her away from the men. "Would you care to tell me what really happened?"

Abigail put her hands to her face as if remembering her shame. "I don't really know for sure myself. My husband is away, and I woke up this morning with a strange man on top of me. I screamed, and these two barged into my room. Then the man ran out while these two tore my robe off of me and dragged me out into the street. I had fought to get away from them, and Joram here," she rubbed at her cheek and pointed at the tunic-clad brother, "knocked me back down and tore at my tunic. He wanted me completely naked when they dragged me out of the house. I felt so ashamed, I didn't even blame him at the time. I just wanted to die in my disgrace. Your words made me realize I must fight, for my son's sake."

"Did you recognize who the man was?"

She shook her head. "No. I'd never seen him before."

"Was it any of these men?"

She stared at each man in turn, but finally shook her head. "No, he was a bit older, with a curly red beard and bushy eyebrows. And I think he smelled rather sickeningly sweet. It made me want to gag."

"But he wasn't any wealthy man from Bethel you know?"

Abigail stared at all of the men. "No. I'd never seen him before in my life. I don't even think he looked Hebrew."

"Interesting," Deborah pursed her lips and turned toward the men. "So you've all lied to me again. What do you have to say for yourselves?"

Hatred gleamed in Joram's eyes. "I say she's a liar and a whore, and you're a fool for listening to one word she says! She's bewitched my *Abba* into believing her beloved-*Adonai* act, but we both saw her with her lover, and if you were a true judge in Israel as you claim, you'd know that the law demands she die for her sin, and we wouldn't be having this conversation because she'd be dead by now!"

"Yeah! Yeah!" All the men with Joram agreed. One of them picked up a large stone and a few others swiftly followed his example.

Deborah moved to stand in front of Abigail. "No! I find no guilt in her! If you touch her, I will bring you all before the elders of Bethel on a charge of murder! You could have come before them, but you didn't. You marched right past them and you came before me. I say your witnesses are not valid. They have cause to hate her, and they have repeatedly lied to me."

A few of Deborah's regular watchers also moved to shield the young woman. When the men finally dropped the stones, she pulled Abigail back to sit in her own chair, further away from them.

"I think you'd better come home with me this evening, and tomorrow my husband and I will go with you to talk with your husband."

"But what about my son?" Abigail cried. "He's only four, and I fear what they will do if I'm not there to protect him."

Deborah looked over to the older students of the law who had been listening attentively. "Can you boys run as quickly as you can to Bethel and explain to the elders in the city gate what's been going on here? Tell them Abigail is innocent of any wrongdoing and her son needs protection from his brothers. Go quickly."

The lads took off. For a while, Deborah simply stood and glared at the group from Bethel. She had to give the boys a good head start before she let the men go. Surprisingly, none of the men dared leave until she said they could. She shook her finger at each of them. "Nothing had better harm her son or my young men of the law. If it does, you will all pay dearly for it. Do you understand that? Now get out of here."

When they had departed, she went back to Abigail. "Here. Let me help you. I think I have some balm for your cheek. Come sit down over here by my son."

"Thank you so much. You don't know how much I appreciate all your help." Abigail took the balm and spread it on her cheek before wrapping Joram's robe tightly around herself and sitting beside Halal. Though she was a stranger to him, he put his little arms tightly around her neck and hugged her. She seemed to immediately relax.

"Deborah, I really didn't understand what was happening until you asked what they had to gain. Then suddenly it all fell into place. But I doubt I can prove it. I just hope my husband believes the truth!"

"I think he will. He must have suspected something bad about them. Why else would he disinherit them in the first place?"

"Because they have forsaken *Adonai*," Abigail whispered. "They love to carouse with the temple priestesses and prostitutes. They even put an *Asherah* pole out in our field. When my husband saw it, he was absolutely furious. He chopped it down immediately, of course. He's not nearly as old or as feeble as they made him out to be. That's when he said he was going to disinherit them. At first, they even tried to blame me for the *Asherah* pole, but when my husband wouldn't believe them, they finally admitted it and used the crop failure as an excuse. Maybe some are truly deceived into believing there is some magic in those things, but for them I know it's for their own perverse pleasure. They must have been planning this for weeks, but waited until their father was away at our other field before they put this plan into action."

She attempted to stand, but her trembling legs threatened to topple her, and even as she touched Deborah's outstretched hand, she sat back down in defeat. "That they would come to you instead of the elders is what confused me. I've heard so much about you. The women of Bethel talk about you all the time as one who truly stands for *Adonai*'s truth. I admired you so much because I knew you were a woman of the law. In Bethel, they call you the Woman of Light. And even though I knew I had done nothing wrong, I felt guilty under the law. I thought I deserved your punishment. I thought *Adonai* and my husband would never forgive me."

CHAPTER 23

For, behold, the wicked bend the bow, they make ready their arrow upon the string to shoot in darkness at the upright in heart. Psalm 11:2

After the men left, Deborah began to shake almost as much as Abigail did. Those men were out to destroy her just as much as they were out to get rid of Abigail. In their eyes, this was an unwinnable case. In cases of adultery, the law clearly called for death by stoning, but after talking with Abigail for only a short time, it was obvious that she was a righteous young woman who loved *Adonai* and both loved and respected her husband. That would also be evident to anyone who knew her. Had Deborah simply followed the law without questioning the motives of the accusers, the women of Bethel would have seriously and rightfully doubted her discernment. Yet, if she had shown mercy without finding the cause, many would also rightly question her commitment to the law. Even now, some would believe the accusation and doubt Deborah's judgment. She couldn't worry about that.

And this wasn't over. First, they had to get Abigail safely to her husband. If he believed her, which wasn't certain, since by the time they got there, his sons surely would have had plenty of time to fill his head with more lies, what would they do then? If his sons were desperate enough to do something this despicable, what else would they do?

"Let's have some lunch," she called out. She turned toward Abigail and lowered her voice. "You must be nearly starving by now, and those ruffians rudely interrupted us before we could have our midday break." She turned back to the crowd still gathered around. "I think we've had enough excitement for one day, so unless anyone has something urgent to discuss, you may all go home and come back tomorrow. I'd especially like to thank those of you who protected this young woman from those who would harm her. May the blessings of *Adonai* be upon each one of you. I do believe that true justice was done here today, and that seems to be a rare occurrence these days."

Many in the crowd cheered their agreement with that assessment, but a couple turned away, grumbling.

As she sat down to open her sack of provisions, Halal tugged at her sleeve. "*Ima*, what's 'dultry'?"

A few of the stragglers heard him and turned and smiled. This they wanted to hear.

"Adultery, son," Deborah corrected, kissing the top of his head. "That's a very good question, but you're a little young to understand the answer. It's when an *Ima* loves another man besides the *Abba*."

"But you love me. Won't you still love me when I'm a man?"

"Of course I will. You're my son. That's different."

"Why?"

"It just is. *Imas* always love their babies. Even when you're old and you're a *Saba* yourself, I'll still love you."

"That's good. And they won't kill you for being adultery?"

"No, Halal, the law knows that *Imas* love their sons."

CHAPTER 24

The commander of his army was Sisera, who lived in Harosheth-hagoyim.
Judges 4:2b

Meanwhile, another mother was comforting her son in Harosheth-hagoyim. "So what if a few pesky Israelites have made some minor raids against your more isolated soldiers, my son? What can they do against nine-hundred iron chariots? Most of them don't even have horses to ride. They hide in trees or lay in wait at the oasis. Just tell Jabin that he must strike now and wipe out these pathetic rebels before they become stronger."

As she spoke, Athtor combed Sisera's magnificent hair and beard, and rained little kisses on his cheeks and forehead. Sisera shook his curls at her, and fell onto the couch, face down.

"Jabin says not yet. We have too many wars going on in too many other places. For now, he just wants me to oppress them mightily; to wear them down bit by bit so that, when the time comes, it won't be much of a battle at all. We'll just sweep in and take what is ours. It's worked in all of his other conquests. All of the other kings of Canaan gave in without much struggle. Now their armies are just another part of ours. Amalek's army is almost as good as we are, but he gave in without a single skirmish. Could you rub my back, Mother? Keeping that big black stallion under control from an iron chariot is so hard on my shoulders. They ache dreadfully."

"I know, my dearest." She kneaded his shoulders like a piece of stubborn bread dough. "Perhaps you should have put him down after he killed that young woman."

"Why would I do that?" He snorted. "He's a great animal, and she was a child of no importance."

Athtor kneaded harder, pouring fragrant oils onto his back and rubbing them in. "Then why do I still hear you cry out in your sleep about it?"

He turned to face her. "I don't know. It doesn't happen as often any more, but I still see her face in my dreams, and it haunts me. I've killed so many men in battle, and I've never had a second thought about it."

"That's just because you have such a kind heart, my son. *Ashtoreth* is very pleased to have you in her service." She kissed him again.

CHAPTER 25

New gods were chosen; Then war was in the gates.
Judges 5:8a

As they were preparing to go home for the day, Barak appeared with six of his men. Deborah of course recognized Joshua, but the rest of them were unfamiliar to her. "Beloved, I wasn't expecting to see you here today. I am always glad for the surprise, but what has brought you?"

"We heard what happened here, and we thought you might need protection going home. Besides, my men could use a good meal in their bellies before they head back for Kedesh. Sisera's army tried to move south toward us again, but we've been able to keep him contained to the northern lowlands. I don't know how much longer that will be true though if we don't get some help."

At that moment, Abigail arrived, pulled along by an overly-excited Halal. "*Abba, Abba,* it is you. I saw the horses coming, and I told *Ima* it was you, but she didn't believe me. She said you were at the olive groves."

"*Ima* was right, but I got back early." He lifted Halal up onto his shoulders, and turned back to Deborah. "The steward says the olives will be ready in about two weeks. It looks like we're going to be fine for this year. The olives seem to be a bit smaller than normal, but I guess that was to be expected."

"Yes." Deborah nodded. "Beloved, this is Abigail. If you heard anything about what happened, you may already know that she is in severe danger from her husband's two sons. They tried to make me believe her guilty of adultery so that I would condemn her to be stoned. I think their plot was as much against me as it was against her, but I'm not sure why. They were trying to discredit me in the eyes of all of Bethel."

Abigail nodded, but even Deborah could barely see her under all the swaths of Deborah's cloth she had wrapped herself in at the approach of the noise of the horses and donkeys. She bowed low. "Blessed be the Name of *Adonai*, and may you be greatly blessed, my lord. You must be Lappidoth, the Torchman, the husband of Deborah. I have heard so much about you. Everyone says you have the best oil in all of Israel. Though we have never met, I have often bought your oil from my local merchant."

"Thank you." At least she had only heard the last part of the conversation. For a long time now, he had been in the habit of introducing himself as Lappidoth, the oil and wick vendor, or as Barak, commander of the rebel forces. It was not time yet for the people to connect Barak to Deborah. It was too dangerous for her and for his children. But it looked like she could get herself into trouble with the opposition even without his help. Word was, the men she had tangled with this morning had been seen collaborating with Sisera's forces.

"Well, I doubt we'll have any problems as long as we're home by sunset."

They were almost home when Joram and his men struck, taking advantage of the lengthening shadows near the city gate. All of them pounced at once, flashing knives and swords they were sadly inept at using. With the element of surprise, they could have inflicted serious damage nevertheless.

But there was no surprise. Barak's men were armed and ready. Within moments, the companions were all dead, and Joram and his brother fled. Joram's brother had been severely wounded, and from the trail of blood, it was doubtful he would live. Barak started to go after them, but Deborah persuaded him it wasn't necessary. Halal needed his bed, and Barak and his men needed to be fed, not out chasing men who would be easily caught in the morning.

It was one of the biggest mistakes Deborah ever made.

CHAPTER 26

Not a shield or a spear was seen among
forty thousand in Israel. Judges 5:8b

"No!" Abigail gasped. "No, how could they?" She stared at the ruins of her home and the charred body of her husband before burying her head in Deborah's embrace. "He was a good father to them. Why would they do this? How could they do this to him?" She began to sob, then panicked again. "Where is Nathan? Where is my son?"

An older woman with streaming gray hair flowing from under her headscarf ran up, panting. "No need to worry about Nathan, my dear." She took Abigail into her own arms. "He is fine. He's safe in Shiloh with my daughter and son-in-law. When those young boys came yesterday and told us the news, we got him out of here as quickly as we could."

She paused to catch her breath. Meanwhile, several other women of Bethel joined her and each took a turn hugging Abigail. The old woman continued chattering. "Unfortunately, no one saw your husband come home. He must have arrived long after sunset and gone straight to bed because we never saw his torch, and I know those vile sons of his didn't come until the middle of the night because they didn't try to escape quietly. They were screaming and shouting such profanities and waving torches as if they were daring us to try to catch them. But it was already too late. By the time we awoke and came running, all we could do was help to put out the fire. We would have warned him; we would have tried to save him, too, if we'd only known he had returned. Please forgive us."

"You haven't done anything to need my forgiveness, Emi," Abigail cried. "You didn't believe their lies about me, and you protected my son. *Adonai* could not have blessed me with any better friends. May His blessing be on every one of you."

The old woman grunted. "As if we would believe one word those scoundrels said! I knew something was not right when I saw them outside the city gate early yesterday morning. They were talking excitedly with a red-haired man with a curly beard. I'd never seen him before, but they gave him a fistful of gold *shekels*. Then later, when my daughter-in-law told me they had dragged you out into the street half-naked to be stoned, I knew these old bones would never get me to Deborah in time to save you. All I could do was fast and pray. And I did. I've never spent so long on my face before *Adonai* before. And He answered my prayers!"

She turned to Deborah and Barak as if suddenly realizing their presence. "Please forgive us for our lack of hospitality. May I get you a cup of wine and some bread? My home is right down this way. I would be honored if you would be my guests. Please come. You may be interested to know, I also heard them laughing bitterly and saying something about at least being so glad they had burned your house down."

Deborah gasped. Things were starting to fall into place. Sair wasn't the only one who had blamed her for the flooding. And things were worse in Bethel because they hadn't learned other skills like her friends in Ramah had. The woman's supply of food would be scant, and she really didn't want to take it, but it would be quite rude to refuse such generous hospitality, so she took the old woman's arm.

"I do believe your prayers saved Abigail's life. From the moment they brought her, I knew something wasn't right. She certainly looked guilty enough, the way they had torn her clothing, and she wouldn't look at me, which is usually a sure sign of guilt, but it was like my spirit was screaming at me not to trust them. I think your prayers did that."

For the first time, the old woman beamed at her. "Blessed be *Adonai* for granting you the wisdom to see beyond your eyes."

Deborah sighed. "You know, I think that can be His greatest gift to us. I just wish I'd had that gift last night when I told my husband and his men not to go after Joram. I thought he'd be so much easier to capture in the daylight, and they needed food and rest for the task. But if they had gone after him, Abigail might have a home and a husband now."

"Or she might not," the old woman shrugged. "In the darkness, they might still have gotten away, and they might even have killed your husband or one of his men in the process. There were several men who came here in the night, so Joram must have had more friends waiting nearby. We cannot always know what might have been. We can only praise *Adonai* for what is."

"Amen," Deborah agreed.

END OF BOOK ONE

BOOK TWO

I will lift up my eyes to the mountains; From where shall my help come? My help comes from the Lord, Who made heaven and earth. Psalm 121:1-2

CHAPTER
1

The chastening for our well-being fell upon Him, and by His scourging we are healed. Isaiah 53:5b

For nearly fifteen years now, Barak had been the General of Israel's army. His little band of two hundred had grown to about five thousand, and they had had some successes in fighting against Sisera. But not nearly enough. He was still the pesky flea that, no matter how much you scratched at it, just wouldn't go away.

Barak was tired. He wanted to go home; to lie in his own bed and be with his own wife for a while. All of his children were grown and had children of their own now. He was the *Saba* to fourteen grandchildren. He had never seen the last two; it wasn't safe. Sisera and Jabin had put a price on Barak's head of a thousand gold *shekels*. These days, even when he traveled as Lappidoth, sometimes it wasn't enough. His face had become too well-known. It was time to quit. *Adonai* could let one of his younger men take over and lead this bunch of cantankerous ungrateful grumblers.

Provisions were getting scarcer all the time. The people wanted protection from Sisera, but they weren't willing to use their own limited resources to provide for the needs of his troops. Some saw them as little better than Sisera in asking for their goods.

If it weren't for that olive grove, how could they have survived? Every year that grove kept producing when almost nothing else did. There were always wicks and oil for the lamps in the Tabernacle, with enough to spare to sell to anyone who had means to pay for it. Many of the wives of his men had gone to work for Deborah, helping in the business. Some of the men of Ramah and Bethel who weren't in the army had also gone to work for them, distributing the oil and wicks and the other merchandise the former tent dwellers of Ephraim had made, not just in Israel, but in much of Egypt and Moab and other surrounding nations that weren't so depleted by the famine. Thus, the faithful in Ephraim who still worshipped *Adonai* had largely escaped the famine and distress much of the rest of Israel had fallen into.

But the task of feeding so many men was daunting at the best of times, and these were certainly not the best. His men were soldiers, not cooks. Even if they had the supplies, how were they supposed to carry them around from place to place and still keep them fresh enough to be edible? Where was the quail? Where was the manna that fell from the sky every day so that all one had to do was pick it up, boil it, and eat it? If the Israelites in the wilderness had grumbled a lot, Barak was sure his men were far worse.

Some of them had taken to stealing sheep from nearby pastures. Tonight, two of them had been caught. They did it because they were hungry though. Barak hated to do it, but he now had to severely discipline them for it. The army of Israel was not a band of thieves!

"Bring the men in."

Joshua led in two younger men Barak had seen a few times in the camp, usually causing trouble. "This is Aholiab," Joshua pointed out the bigger one who was almost as tall as Joshua himself, but as thin as a tent peg. "And that's Jubal. They're both from the tribe of Zebulun, and they've only been here a few weeks.

They're the ones who decided to have lamb stew for dinner. They didn't even properly slaughter the animal so that the whole thing could be eaten; just killed it, took what they wanted and left the rest for the jackals to devour."

The waste was a bigger crime than the theft. A whole lamb could have made enough stew to serve half his men.

"Has the shepherd set a price?"

"No. He's plenty angry, but he'll take whatever you decide."

If only Deborah were here. She would know so much better how to deal with this. Other countries he'd heard about might have the right idea: they cut off the hands of the thieves they caught. The law of Israel didn't allow that. Under the law, these two needed to make restitution or be sold into slavery for up to six years for their crime.

He looked them over grimly. Their tunics and robes weren't much more than tattered remnants. There was no way they could pay. Slavery was the only answer. But weren't they already slaves to Israel, in a way? As their commander, wasn't it his responsibility to provide food for them so that they wouldn't feel the need to steal? He had provided food, but obviously it wasn't enough for them.

He sighed. "Joshua, bring my money bag!"

Joshua did as Barak had commanded, and brought him a goatskin bag with a leather strip laced through and tied around the edge to draw it tightly closed. He lifted out four large gold nuggets and weighed them in his palm. "Even at double the value, this should be enough. Take it to the shepherd with my sincere apologies and assurances it will never happen again. And then post a guard to see that it doesn't. And put this back where you found it, please. We have more food coming in the morning, and I'll need this to pay for it. And issue a warning to the men that any further stealing will be immediately punishable by death! I will not have an army of thieves!"

After Joshua left, Barak continued to stare at the two for a long while, drumming his fingertips on his knee. "As for you two, I sentence you each to ten lashes. But as your commander, I feel that it is my responsibility to pay all the penalties for your crime, not just the financial ones, so this evening I will be stripped of my tunic, and Joshua will deliver to me twenty lashes in front of all the men."

"No, Commander," Aholiab gasped, "you needn't do that. We'll take our own punishment."

Jubal nodded his agreement to Aholiab's assertion.

"No," Barak sighed. "This way perhaps you will remember that your actions reflect on me and every other man in this camp, and in the future you will choose them more wisely. As long as you stay here in this troop, you may consider yourselves to be my servants. You will go where I say go, do what I say do, and become the kind of soldiers *Adonai* meant for you to be. I'll have no more of your foolish troublemaking! You have been bought with a price. Yet you are not my slaves. You may leave this camp and return to your home at any time you wish. But know this. Whether or not you're still in my army, if I ever hear of you doing anything like this again, I will personally gut you just like you gutted that sheep!"

He leaned closer, and put his face up against each of theirs. "And don't think I didn't see you both eying that moneybag earlier. Don't even think about it. If I catch you trying to steal it, and believe me, I will catch you, the law gives me the freedom to do whatever I will to you. Do you both understand me?"

"Yes, Commander," said the one called Aholiab.

Jubal merely nodded meekly.

At sunset, Barak did just as he had said. Joshua, with tears running down his own face the whole time, delivered the twenty lashes to his beloved commander.

CHAPTER 2

You shall love the Lord your God with all your heart and with all your
soul and with all your might.
Deuteronomy 6:5

Tears streamed down Deborah's cheeks as Halal packed his gear, kissed his wife and newborn baby, and prepared to mount up to join his father at the camp.

"Please come back," she cried. "I have already lost one child, and I don't think I could bear it to lose another. Remember when you were little, and you asked me was it adultery for a mother to love her son? Maybe I was wrong. Maybe it is adultery against *Adonai* to love our sons so much that we couldn't bear to lose them, even in His service. If so, I guess I'm guilty. My heart is breaking right now at the mere thought of it."

Halal, who was so much the image of his father, came over and put his strong arms around her shoulders. "No, *Ima*," he kissed her wrinkled cheek. "You were absolutely right. *Adonai* does understand mothers. You are the way you are because He made you with immense hearts full of love that could encompass all your children as well as your husband and any others who might cross your path, but your first love will always be Him. If it weren't, you wouldn't be able to love the rest of us nearly as well. Don't worry about me. I am in the hand of *Adonai*, and what better place could I be? You and *Abba* have taught me well."

He turned and kissed his sisters and each of their children farewell before he again kissed his wife and baby, and climbed up on the gray donkey. "Please care for my wife and daughter. If *Adonai* is willing, I will see you all again by *Pesach*."

With that, he began, as always, to sing with his deeply resonant voice, a song of praise to *Adonai* for His goodness.

Deborah turned away. It hurt too much to watch him ride off. A voice inside her told her she would never see Halal again in this life. But she wouldn't say that out loud. Words had power, and she didn't want to give this thought any power. Perhaps she was wrong. Perhaps *HaSatan* was merely tormenting her with such an evil thought. She walked over to her daughter-in-law and took her granddaughter into her arms and hugged her weeping daughter-in-law.

"Come," she urged all her daughters, "It's so delightful to have you all here together again, even if it is for such a sad occasion. But let's not dwell on that. Let's get busy. These children need something to eat, and it isn't going to make itself. While we work, tell me the news. What is new in each of your lives? It seems I haven't seen my beautiful daughters in such a long time!"

CHAPTER 3

Are they not finding, are they not dividing the spoil? A maiden, two maidens for every warrior. Judges 5:30a

At Harosheth-hagoyim, Athtor was also busy. She had a gift for her son Sisera: another Hebrew girl his army had taken captive. She had already bathed the girl in jasmine and myrrh-scented water. Now she vigorously brushed and braided the girl's hair and perfumed her body. This one should do fairly well. She had the slender body and smooth skin that Sisera preferred, and her long hair and dark eyes should please him. How good a lover she would be remained to be seen, but it didn't really matter much. He would train her to please him in that regard. If he didn't kill her first.

"Tell me your name, girl."

"Lilith."

"Well, I'd advise you, Lilith, that whatever it is he wants, do it without question, if you want to have any hope of living. My son is a man of strong appetites which are not easily quenched." Her eyes gleamed. "You will make it much easier on yourself if you relax and enjoy it. You may be surprised to find he is a remarkable lover."

The girl's lips trembled. "But I've never had a lover. I am a virgin of Israel. My betrothed would have come for me at any time. Please don't let your son do this to me. Please help me!"

Athtor smiled. A bonus. The girl was a virgin. Sisera would like that. "Listen, girl. Don't be stupid. Your days as a virgin of Israel are over and gone. You will be lucky if you become known as the harlot of Israel. At least then you'll be alive."

The girl began to weep.

"Stop that. Sisera hates weakness. I'm trying to help you here. You do you want to live, don't you?"

The girl shrugged. "I'm not sure. Perhaps it would be better if I died now in my purity. Then at least I might stand clean before *Adonai* at His judgment seat."

"Don't talk nonsense, girl. If you live, you can always go to your *Adonai* for forgiveness later, can't you? I thought that was supposed to be the advantage you Hebrews had over the rest of us. All you have to do is go burn a poor innocent lamb, and all is forgiven. If you're dead, there's no lamb that can bring you back, is there? Here, put this on, and sit here while I make up your face. I want you to be beautiful when Sisera gets here. At least our goddess *Ashtoreth* only desires our fertility rites. I could teach you her ways if you like. Then you could dance for my son, and have him under your spell for the rest of his life. And it just might guarantee your own life too."

The girl shuddered, then sighed, as if considering it.

CHAPTER 4

He who goes about as a slanderer reveals secrets,
therefore do not associate with a gossip. Proverbs 20:19

Since the lashing, Aholiab and Jubal had been well-behaved. Who knew that taking a beating would make for such loyal servants? And it turned out that the stealth they had used in stealing the sheep was a great asset when they put it to use as spies against Sisera.

Jubal did indeed have a voice, and was an excellent observer and listener, attributes extremely valuable in a spy. Not only that, but he could speak and understand several languages, something the enemy might not be expecting, and which could make them extremely careless in their loose talk around their campfires.

"Commander, he's at home at Harosheth-hagoyim now," Jubal reported. "They say he may be there several days since they know his mother acquired him a new maiden to be his concubine, and they think it will take at least that long for the sport of it to wear off."

As Barak frowned at this news, Jubal hurried to continue. "And Jabin is in Hazor with his wives and concubines. The troops at Shechem are vulnerable. The man they left in charge is young and inexperienced at command. Their army is as tired and hungry as ours was. At least until tonight." He grinned. "Sir, I hope your ban on stealing sheep didn't apply to Sisera's sheep. Aholiab and I brought back a couple. The men are making lamb stew as we speak."

Barak laughed. "No, it didn't apply to Sisera's sheep at all. My back is safe and so are you. You have my permission to take as many of them as you can carry. He probably stole them from our lands in the first place. Good work. Joshua will be happy you brought back the whole sheep this time. I think that's what made him the maddest last time. As soon as the men eat, tell Joshua to have them prepare to head out. We're heading toward Shechem. Tonight!"

"Yes, sir. But you may want to know, your son just rode into camp. I'd never met him, but I heard some of the men say he was your son. I think he must be pretty tired by now. You may want to wait until morning to leave."

"No. If my son is too tired, he can catch up to us tomorrow. We need to move now."

CHAPTER 5

*Yet your desire will be for your husband,
and he will rule over you. Genesis 3:16b*

Jael stirred her cooking pot, and peered into her huge iron oven. She had a lamb roasting, lentils, onions, and leeks stewing, fig cakes and honey, pomegranates, dates, cucumbers and olives. That should be enough. She felt the wineskin. It was less than half-full. Better get a new one.

Heber was having guests tonight. He so loved to entertain. But his choice of guests was sometimes a problem. He had made peace with Jabin, and with Sisera. He said it was for the best; that it would protect her and their children from both sides. She gazed into the tiny face of her baby. After so long being barren, *Adonai* had given her a beautiful little baby girl with springy curls and big eyes with lots of thick eyelashes. She had named her Rachel.

At night, in her dreams, she could still see the face of her friend Rachel as she was crushed under the foot of that black stallion. And she could see the face of the driver of that chariot too. It was years before she had known that it was the face of Sisera. She had no doubt of it at all. But who would believe her? Who would even care? A girl was valueless to most. Sisera probably didn't even remember.

At least Sisera wasn't the guest tonight. It was just some minor official of Jabin's court and his guards. Jael had met him before. He had leered at her like she was a piece of the roast lamb and he intended to devour her. And that was when she was great with child. He might be even more aggressive now. Hopefully, this time he would bring a wife or a concubine to keep him busy and his eyes off her.

Heber was a blessing as a husband. He was kind, and polite, and always good to her. But he always wanted to make everybody happy. He hated quarreling of any kind. That was a good thing in a husband. But was it always a good thing in the eyes of *Adonai*? Heber tended to make compromises. He didn't mind having the little statues of *Baal* and *Ashtoreth* around their home. He said they didn't believe in them, so what difference did it make? All that was important was that it made Jabin and Sisera happy and comfortable here. Of course, he always put them away whenever he knew Barak or Deborah or any of their Hebrew friends were expected. All Jael could do about it was ask *Adonai* to forgive her and remind Him that He had commanded her to obey her husband.

The official's name was Beliel, and he hadn't brought his wife or his concubine. Every time Heber glanced away, Beliel seemed to stare at her more lewdly. "Your certainly are a blessed man, Heber," he said, licking his lips. "You have a wife who takes care of all your needs. She cooks like one of the king's best butchers, and she's a feast to the eyes as well."

Heber took it as a compliment, of course. "Yes, you're right. I am. You should be so blessed to find such a wife for yourself, Beliel."

"Thank you, my friend. But there aren't many around like Jael. She still has a figure like a maiden. Most of the women of Hazor have figures like *Ashtoreth* after they have a child. It rather sickens me. Truthfully, I like them young enough they still have that rather boyish figure with only enough shape to them to know they aren't boys."

He leaned forward to whisper to Heber. "Sisera's got himself one like that right now. Just seeing her makes me drool like a thirsty camel. He's taking her day and night. He can't get enough of her. It's funny. She reminds me a lot of Jael. If I didn't know better, I'd swear they were sisters."

Beliel and Heber didn't realize Jael had overheard their conversation, and Heber hadn't at all gotten the obvious hint that she was also a subject of the fool's camel drool.

CHAPTER 6

Do not urge me to leave you or turn back from following you. Ruth 1:16

Nathan hugged his mother. Abigail was still young-looking despite having now buried two husbands. Although most of the women of Bethel loved her, some considered her cursed of *Adonai* since she had never had any more children after she had been accused of adultery by her first husband's two sons. They believed that somehow that proved the truth of the accusation.

"*Ima*, you know I need to go. Israel needs me. Perhaps this is the reason I was spared all those years ago."

Abigail paced their little home in Bethel. It wasn't far from her first home, and she had felt so blessed to have it. Nathan had always been such a wonderful son, so like his father in his devotion to *Adonai* and his fierce love of justice and kindness. He was not at all given to aggressive behavior like most of the boys his age.

"But you're still too young," she pleaded. "You haven't had a chance to have a wife and son yet. You could go next year, after the barley harvest. Then you would be old enough and, in the meantime, you could take a wife, and give me a grandson so that if anything happens to you in the battle, I will not be left alone. The law allows it. Even Deborah would tell you that. Her son only left to join his father a few days ago, and he is almost three years older than you are. Why must you go so soon?"

"I don't know," he admitted. "I just know I must. It's like I hear a small voice inside that says, 'go now'. "

"And does this voice also tell you how to find them? They hide in the hills. You could look for weeks and not know where to find Barak and his men."

He laughed. "That's the easy part. I heard in the gate yesterday that there is a legion of Sisera's army camping at Shechem. If Barak hears about them, he'll go there, too. I won't be alone. Some of the other men of Bethel are also going."

Abigail laughed through her tears. The men he was talking about were boys just like he was, barely past their *bar mitzvah*, and eager for a taste of battle, but unprepared for the realities of war. "So you've made up your mind? All right. Then I'm going too."

This time it was Nathan's turn to be aghast. "What? *Ima*, no! Women don't go to war! You need to stay here where it's safe!"

"There is no safe place in Israel right now, son. I've lost two husbands, and all I have left in this world is one son. I don't intend to lose him. I don't know what I'll be able to do to help, but surely they need someone who can bandage up the wounded and cook meals for the men, and comfort the dying."

"But *Ima*, it's a bunch of men who have no women. It wouldn't be safe for you there."

Abigail bent to inspect her stores of provisions to see what could reasonably be carried with them. There was no need to go empty-handed. "I'm sure General Barak can control his men. Neither you nor he would let anything harm me. And even if it does, as you said, perhaps it's the reason I was spared all those years ago. I'm coming. It's settled."

CHAPTER 7

For wisdom is better than jewels; and all desirable things cannot compare with her. Proverbs 8:11

Athtor strode into the large bedroom. Silk curtains tied back with gold cords revealed piles of cushions of scarlet and purple with rope tassels that served as Sisera's massive bed. She stared down her nose at the young woman who lay reclining there, playing with all the pots of cosmetics provided for her. "So, you think you have my son right where you want him now, do you? You would have the audacity to try to get him to send me away? Me! I am his mother. I will not be ordered out by a little harlot like you! How dare you?!"

Lilith put down the pot of kohl and grinned smugly, not even bothering to get up. "If I'm a harlot, it's because you taught me how to be one. Thank you for that. As you predicted, my Sisera is a wonderful lover."

Finally, she stood and walked gracefully over to Athtor, the little bells of her silken veils tinkling as she walked. "I please Sisera.

I just told him we could have a lot more pleasure if his mother weren't always around to interfere with his activities."

"Why you…" Athtor reached to grab her by the little gold ring that hung from her nose but Lilith backed away just in time. "You think you can't be replaced? I'll have you butchered and sent back to your tribe in pieces for this! You think I won't? There are hundreds just like you waiting to take your place! Sisera would never even notice your absence!"

The fierceness of her threat and the probable truth of her words worked their intent on Lilith. She gasped. "Would you slaughter your own grandchild?"

"You're pregnant?" Athtor's anger evaporated and her face drained of its color.

"I think so. I haven't had the way of women since I've been here, and I wake feeling sick to my stomach."

Athtor turned her back to her. "Then you're the one we need to get out of here right now."

"Why? Wouldn't Sisera be delighted to know he's to be a father?"

"No, of course not, you fool! My son doesn't like his women pregnant. The moment he realizes it, he will kill both you and the child!" She smiled a wicked smile. "Of course if you really want to stay here, I can give you something to get rid of the baby. I have plenty of *Ashtoreth's* potions. That's easily enough taken care of!"

Lilith gasped. "No! I know I have greatly offended *Adonai* by being with Sisera, but I cannot and will not take the life of my own child! His law says not to murder!"

Athtor smiled to herself. This one had really worried her. Sisera had asked her to leave his house so he could be with this one. Never had he done that before. Somehow, she would find a way to get the girl back to her people. If they killed her because of her condition, so be it, but at least she wouldn't be the one to kill her own grandchild.

CHAPTER 8

But the path of the righteous is like the light of dawn,
that shines brighter and brighter until the full day. Proverbs 4:18

"*Shalom*, Halal!" Nathan called to his friend. "I didn't expect to see you before I reached your father's camp!"

Halal turned from his game of pitching nuts at a hole in a tree about fifty cubits from him and embraced his friend. He and Nathan had studied the law with Deborah since they were young boys, so Nathan was like his little brother. "*Shalom*, my friends," he nodded to Abigail and the rest of the boys in the group. "May the blessings of *Adonai* be on each one of you. I hadn't expected to see you here either. Why are you going to father's camp? I'm on my way there."

Halal grinned. "I had just stopped to eat and rest a few moments. But I really should hurry. He was expecting to engage Sisera's army soon when I last saw him, so it will not be safe for you there. If you have some provisions for him, I will take them to him. You should go home as quickly as possible."

"We've come to fight, too!" Nathan announced proudly. As Halal glanced at Abigail, Nathan whispered, "*Ima* was determined to follow me. She says she will cook for the men and bandage their wounds. I couldn't persuade her to stay at home."

Halal's mother was often stubborn too, but this time, maybe Abigail's stubbornness would get her killed. He agreed with her though that Nathan was too young to go to war; he didn't yet have a son to care for his mother in her old age. "But you are too young yet to be fighting against Sisera. You must go back home with your mother. You can come back next year. You haven't yet given a wife a son to carry on your name!"

"Neither have you! You only have a daughter!"

Halal nodded. "Yes, I know that, but my *Ima*'s *Saba* gave a word to *Abba* that Jacob's prophecy to Naphtali was about my *Ima*; that she would give birth to beautiful fawns. She had prayed and He made an exception in my case, but when my daughter was born, I knew that it would be the only exception. There will be no son. So there is no reason for me not to go to war."

Nathan nodded. "I'm not to wait either. *Adonai* spoke to me in a dream the other night. He said I was to rise up and go immediately. He has a task for me."

"Really? *Adonai* spoke to you? You're not just saying that to get to go to camp early?" He examined Nathan's small boyish face for any signs of deception. He found none.

Nathan was exuberant. His smile was guileless and infectious. "No, I swear it. I had intended to go next year, just as *Ima* had wanted, but the dream was quite real. I saw the angel of the Lord, and He spoke to me as clearly as you just did."

Halal's eyes widened. "Wow! What did He look like?"

Nathan's face lit up even more. "He was big and a bright light shone all around Him that was almost blinding in its strength. He had beautiful brown eyes that held my own gaze although I felt the need to bow my face to the ground in worship. His smile warmed me through with such joy. It was like a fire on a cold night. It wasn't like a dream at all. I will never forget it."

Halal had no doubt that Nathan had indeed seen the Angel of the Lord. "So what are you to do?"

Nathan frowned. "I don't know yet. He didn't tell me. He just said go. I wanted so badly to ask Him more, but He vanished as quickly as He had come."

Halal put his arm around Nathan's shoulder. "Then let us go together. We should reach my father's camp by sunset easily. Tomorrow is *Shabbat*, so they will not be fighting."

"Let's just hope Sisera will honor *Shabbat*," Nathan reminded him.

CHAPTER 9

But the seventh day is a Sabbath of the Lord your God; in it you shall not do any work, you or your son or your daughter, your male or your female servant or your cattle or your sojourner who stays with you. Exodus 20:10

Abigail awoke in Barak's camp the next morning with a sense of triumph. After a lengthy discussion, she had finally convinced Barak to let her stay. Of course, he had given her dire warnings that he couldn't be responsible for her safety. She had to laugh. That was right after he had issued a direct command that anyone who dared to harm her would personally answer to him with their life forfeited to his blade. It hadn't hurt her case that as they were talking a soldier came back to camp severely injured from a fall off a steep hill, and Abigail had quickly and easily set and bandaged his broken and badly cut leg. Having an adventurous but sometimes rather clumsy son did have its advantages. Abigail had become known in Bethel for her healing abilities, and had treated many of population for their injuries over the years. Those skills would come in handy now.

"Baruch atah Adonai Eloheinu Melech ha-olam, asher kidshanu m'mitzvotav v'tzivanu l'hadlik ner shel Shabbat."

Since it was the *Sabbath*, there were no fires lit in the camp other than the *Sabbath* light, and she shivered with cold, but Abigail listened as Barak gave the *Shabbat* blessing and a short word of encouragement to his men. They were far away from the tabernacle, and they had no priests or Levites in the camp. He asked his men to remember that the *Sabbath* was a precious gift given to Israel by *Adonai* Himself. They should use it wisely to examine their lives and remember those things that were important to them; most importantly, *Adonai* Himself, then their wives, their children, their parents, and their homes. These were the things they were on this mountainside to protect. What *Adonai* had given them was also precious to Him, and if it was worth having, it was worth protecting, even with their lives if necessary.

It wasn't a long speech, but few of the long-winded orators of Bethel could have done better. After that, the men sang a portion of the Song of Moses, and recited their own prayers as Barak had instructed them. It was a privilege to be among a group of devoted followers of *Adonai*. It often seemed that so many had fallen away. It was easy to forget that there were still many who loved and served Him with fervor.

It was at the breeze before sunset that trouble began brewing. Abigail had just finished eating her cold supper. No cooking was allowed on the *Sabbath*, so everyone had eaten portions they had saved from the day before. Of course, she had been allowed to tend to the wounded soldier. That was considered a *mitzvah*, which was allowed even on the *Sabbath*. She had often said *Adonai* didn't include wives and mothers in the commandment for no work because He was so wise He knew such a demand was impossible. Children always needed their *Ima* to do something for them, whether it was to kiss a boo-boo, or mend a broken leg. And husbands and soldiers were no different. It was as she was going to check on the injured man, that she heard them.

"They're just the other side of the range. I saw their signal fires. They don't keep the *Sabbath* like we do. If we ride now, we could be there by the second watch. We'd catch them while they were sleeping, and it wouldn't be much of a fight. I don't think there are very many of them. But the group they were signaling is much bigger. I saw lots of fire there, and they're not that far away. We don't want to give them time to get to the first group."

Barak shook his head. "No, we will not break the *Sabbath*. Tell the men to sleep now. We will ride out at dawn. We should be there shortly before noonday. Maybe, if we're blessed, the first group will be going to the second group, not the other way around. Either way, they won't go until dawn so if we meet them halfway, we may still have the advantage. We know they're there."

"Unless they were signaling them that they had spotted us," the soldier warned. "Then they'll be the ones getting here by the second watch."

"Good point! Joshua, you'd better post a guard. If he sees even a flutter of a leaf, I want this whole camp up and armed in the blink of an eye."

"Yes, Commander! We'll be ready!"

CHAPTER 10

Train up a child in the way he should go, even when he is old he will not depart from it. Proverbs 22:6

Chesed came over the next hill toward Deborah's palm tree. Deborah hadn't seen Chesed in quite a while. What could be bringing her out to the judgment chair today? There were already quite a few people gathered about for judgment, but Deborah was having trouble keeping her mind on anything but the sight of Chesed. Did she have news of Joshua and Barak?

Deborah gazed at the parade of children with Chesed. All four of them were the very image of Joshua, big boned with chubby cheeks and ruddy complexions, and with the massive heads of hair which seemed to always defy a comb or head covering. Yet the children also had their mother's smile and the dimples in her cheeks that gave them a more classic beauty. Eliab, her oldest, and the son of the evil Jacob, wasn't with her today. Had he also gone to join Barak? Was that why Chesed had come?

When she arrived, she stayed at the back of the crowd as Deborah rendered decision after decision. Finally, the last case came before Deborah, and was dispatched with ease.

She held out her hands. "Chesed, I am so pleased to see you and all your beautiful children. Blessed be *Adonai* for your continued good health. Have you had word of Joshua?"

Chesed shook her head. "No, not for a good while now, but I take that as good news. I'd hear soon enough if anything bad had happened."

Deborah studied her. "But something is bothering you. Your countenance lacks its usual bright smile. And you wouldn't march all your children all the way out here just to watch my cases." She glanced at the oldest boy. "Is Benjamin old enough to begin studying the law?"

Chesed laughed and rubbed Benjamin's massive tangle of hair. "Almost," she agreed, "but I'm not sure he has the temperament for it. I know you're a great teacher, but it's rather hard to get him to sit still long enough to even memorize one commandment, much less to study the law. He's like Joshua in that regard. Joshua loves *Adonai* with all his heart, but I know he's happier as a soldier than he ever was as a farmer."

"Then…"

Chesed shooed her children off to play on the mountainside. "Jacob's father died, and Eliab has inherited his estate."

"That's normal," Deborah said. "Jacob was…"

"I know, but we'd never told Eliab about his birth. It just seemed better that way. He'd met his grandparents, of course, but at the time, he didn't really understand who they were. Eliab has always been such a good boy. He was nothing at all like his father. I'll admit it was hard at first, but I did come to love him. He was such a sweet baby, I couldn't help but love him. And Joshua and his parents always treated him exactly like they treated the rest of the children. Eliab has always adored Joshua. When he was little, he practically lived on his *Abba*'s shoulders. Any time Joshua was home, they were inseparable."

Chesed had told this to Deborah many times. What had changed? "But now...?"

Chesed sighed. "Now he's angry. He blames Joshua and me for Jacob's death. He's taken Jacob's side in the argument. He said I didn't have any right to refuse to marry Jacob, and if Joshua had been a real *mensch*, and I'd been a respectful daughter and wife, his father would be alive today."

"Didn't you tell him about..."

"No," she cried. "I couldn't do that to him. If he knew how evil his father really was, it might kill him."

"Or it might bring him to his senses," Deborah reminded her. "Somehow in his heart, Eliab must already feel that truth. That's what's making him so angry. He's fighting against it, and it's causing him to lash out at you and at Joshua, and most of all at *Adonai*. But the one he's most angry at is himself for who he is. He's afraid he will be like his father. Truth can never be hidden for long. It has a strange way of always making its way into the light."

Deborah hugged Chesed. "Now that he knows who he is, it is time for Eliab to decide for himself what kind of man he will be. The anger will fade. The truth will remain. Will all the love you and Joshua have given him be strong enough to overcome his father's evil nature? I don't know the answer to that. I don't think Eliab knows yet. But he will. *Adonai* will test him, and he will soon know."

CHAPTER 11

He who trusts in his riches will fall, but the righteous will flourish like the green leaf. Proverbs 11:28

Eliab had never known such luxury as met his eyes at his grandfather's estate in Kedesh. It was a palace really, at least compared to his home in Bethel. It had a red domed roof and the shuttered windows were like those on Barak and Deborah's house, but it wasn't made of the usual mud brick. It gleamed like gold in the bright sunlight.

How had *Ima* been so foolish as to give up this home for a hovel with Joshua? His father must have been really blessed of *Adonai*. There were at least six or seven camels and a like number of donkeys. There were even two chariots like the ones Sisera's army used, only without the iron scythes or heavy iron sides that guarded riders from weaponry. These were simply designed for speed and pleasure. He couldn't wait to drive one.

As he entered through the front door, a servant greeted and bowed to him, took off his sandals, and washed his feet. Then an old woman he vaguely recognized as having met when he was younger came and kissed him on the cheek, offered him an embroidered silken robe and led him to an inner courtyard where a feast with lamb, wine, grapes, olives, pomegranates, figs, dates, lentils and cheeses was set up. A celebration of his arrival? He couldn't remember the last time he had seen so much food.

Yet every day brought just as much food. He was also given several new robes and tunics, a new *tallith*, and a new *kippah*. And, of course, he was bathed in a scented bath by young servant who offered herself for his pleasure. He declined the offer, at least for the moment. *Ima* wouldn't approve.

All of *Adonai*'s rituals and blessings and holy ordinances were strictly observed in the house. Yet Eliab had never felt so cold or so far from *Adonai*. Even his *Safta*, after that first kiss, was remote and seemingly lost in her own thoughts with no room for him. Still, everywhere he went, the townsmen bowed to him and curried his favor. Women and wine were pushed at him as if they were his due as the master of the house. Perhaps one didn't really need to seek favor from *Adonai* when gold *shekels* could produce the same effect.

CHAPTER 12

Sustain me with raisin cakes, refresh me with apples, because I am lovesick. Song of Solomon 2:5

Athtor counted out the gold *shekels* and tossed them onto the bed. "Give two of these to each of the men who take you to the Kishon River when you arrive safely there. I have arranged for two other men to meet you there and take you down the river to your home. Give each of them two *shekels* too, but only when you reach your home. The rest are for you and the child. You'll need something to get you started. If your people won't accept you, and I tend to doubt they will, you know how you can make your living. But after you become great with child, you may need these to sustain you until the child comes. Just don't let any of the men see how many *shekels* you have with you. These are supposed to be some of Sisera's best men, but I don't know how trustworthy they are. If they give you any trouble, I suppose you could always seduce them as you seduced my son. I cannot guarantee your safety, but if you stay, I can guarantee you'll die, so the choice is up to you."

Lilith snatched up the *shekels*. "Why are you helping me? I know you hate me. You taught me how to please your son, and then you were angry that I did it too well. Why would you help me now?"

Athtor shrugged. "A soothsayer once told me that my descendants would study Torah in Jerusalem, but I don't have any descendants. Sisera has killed them all. Every time one of his women gets pregnant, he kills them and rips the baby right out of their belly. I love my son. Can you understand that? He is a beautiful example of manhood, and I don't want him to be the last of his lineage. I want my grandson to live. If that means letting you live too, so be it. Now, get out of here before he comes home and finds you."

Trembling, Lilith wrapped herself in the warm cloak Athtor had brought her. It was heavy and itchy, far different from the silken finery in Sisera's home, but more suitable for the journey. "Won't he come after me?"

Athtor laughed a high-pitched, shrieking laugh. "No, I don't think so. He may not even notice you're gone. I have a new toy for him to play with. That should keep him distracted for a while — at least long enough for you to get away."

Pangs of jealousy seized Lilith. Sisera would kill her without thought. Why should she feel jealous that he would take another lover? Yet she ached with the knowledge that she did. Athtor was right. He was an excellent lover. She had never known such euphoria. He was never gentle. But he hadn't hurt her either. And her baby would never know his father.

Sisera strode into his mother's bedroom. She was playing with the cosmetics pots she had given to Lilith. She streaked some of the kohl across her eyelid.

"Mother, where is Lilith? There's a strange new harlot in my bed. You know I don't want anyone else besides Lilith. What have you done with her? I need to say goodbye. I have to leave. Jabin has recalled me to the battle."

Athtor tried to look innocent. "She's escaped, son. She's gone back to her people. Maybe you'll meet her there when you get to her home. I'm told she lives down near the Kishon River. Even if you don't, once you take over Israel, you can have as many of their virgins as you like. I'm sure you can find at least one that will please you. You won't even remember her." She reached out to stroke his neck the way he'd always liked.

But he would have none of it tonight. He grabbed her by the arm and twisted it behind her back, moving closer to her.

"Why would she do that?" He snarled against her neck. "There's absolutely nothing left for her in Israel. Their god sees her as damaged goods now. She wouldn't leave me. She's not that stupid." He pushed Athtor away.

Then he began to weep. "They would turn her into a harlot for her adultery with me. That is, if they don't stone her first. I would have taken care of her for the rest of her life. I would have even married her if that's what she wanted. Why did she leave me?"

Athtor rubbed her aching arm. "Don't be a fool, my son. She left because she's pregnant, and I told her you would rip the child right out of her belly after you had killed her for it!"

Sisera gasped. "What? No! Mother, why would you say such a cruel thing? You know I've wanted a child of my own for ages. I would have treated her like a queen! If she'd asked, I could have made her a queen. My men would have followed me even against Jabin himself."

This time Athtor moved behind him and whispered, "That's exactly why she had to go! She'd bewitched you so, you would have done anything she asked. She would have sent me away, and you would have let her do it. She would have taken you from me. None of the rest of them has ever been able to do that. I couldn't let it happen now. You were my precious baby boy. I'll share you, but I'll never let you go."

The sons of Israel cried to the Lord; for he had nine hundred iron chariots.
Judges 4:3

It was late afternoon by the time Barak and his men caught up to the first legion of Sisera's troops. They were indeed headed toward the second legion, but it seemed they were both headed back to Kedesh. Something was up. He had never seen so many signal fires! They seemed to have no notion that Barak and his men were right behind them. Was his little battalion heading for a trap? Why else would they act so oblivious?

Yet Barak obviously took them by surprise, and they won an easy victory with very few casualties on their own side. Joshua and his other lieutenants urged him to go on directly toward the second legion and strike again before the second legion knew they were coming. Something told Barak in his spirit that would be a wrong move. After plundering as many weapons and horses as he could, and a few sheep and some supplies, he ordered his men back up into the mountains to go the roundabout way to Kedesh. As usual, the men grumbled, but they complied.

After sunset, the valley was full of campfires. It seemed that Jabin had brought all nine hundred of his chariots. The second legion wasn't one lone legion. It was Jabin's entire army! If they had ridden toward the second legion, they would have met slaughter!

As she prayed for Barak and his men, like she did every night before sleeping, Deborah had the vision. It was more vivid than any she had ever had in her life. She could see all of Sisera's soldiers, with their grand horses and chariots. The men laughed and bragged about their sexual conquests as well as their envy of their commander's conquests as they played their games of chance. She could even smell the smoke of their campfires. It was as if she walked among them but without them seeing or hearing her.

"Please, no, *Adonai*, help Barak, help Israel, please! I know we have failed You. I know we have forsaken Your ways, and we don't deserve Your help. But the men in that army have not forsaken You. They would serve You with their last breath. *Adonai*, dead men cannot praise You. They cannot serve You at all. Please help them! Tell me what must they do?!"

That's when she heard Him. The voice wasn't audible like the voices of the men in the camp had been in the vision. It was inside of her, yet she could hear it just as plainly as she heard the soldiers. It was real. She knew the voice. She had been listening to it since she was a small girl. It was *Adonai*.

He said, "Tell Barak to take ten thousand men from the sons of Naphtali and from the sons of Zebulun. They are to march to Mt. Tabor. There I will draw Sisera and his chariots to the Kishon River and give him into Barak's hand. Then you will both sing a song of praise to my Name that will be heard in Israel for all time to come."

CHAPTER 14

That the leaders led in Israel, that the people volunteered, Bless the Lord!
Judges 5:2

At dawn, Deborah pounded on the door of Sair's house.

Finally, his second wife came to the door. She snapped as she unlocked and pulled the door open, "Yes, what is it?"

She stopped short when she saw Deborah with her head bared and bare feet in the winter cold. The customary greetings were forgotten. Fear grew on her face; one of Sair's sons was with Barak.

Deborah tried to give her a reassuring smile. "May I come in?"

She stepped in before the question was answered. "No, before you ask, I haven't had any word from the camp. As far as I know they're still fine. But I need to speak with Sair. We need to get a message to Barak as quickly as possible. I was hoping your younger son could take it."

When the woman started to protest, Deborah held up her hand to stop her. "Yes, I know he's not quite old enough yet to go to the army. I'm not asking that. All I want is for him to deliver a message and come straight home. I wouldn't ask, but this is extremely important. Please get Sair."

He walked in, smothering a large yawn. "She doesn't need to. I'm here. Why do you need Abel?"

As Sair ushered her into their front room, seated himself in his cushions, and bade his wife to light the oil lamps, Deborah told him her vision. Did he believe her? Flickers of the old Sair shone on his face. But as she described the hundreds of horses, and the shiny scythes on the chariots, and the soldiers with their games of chance, he began to bob his head up and down.

"So Jabin has finally brought in all of his troops, has he? I've been waiting for this to happen for twenty years. I can't imagine why he's waited this long. We would have been easy pickings twenty years ago when we had no army or such a great leader like your husband has turned out to be. Jabin was a fool to wait so long. *Adonai* has been good to us in spite of our wickedness! Yes, my son will go, but I'm going with him. I'm an old man, and I've never seen war before, but I will stand with my countrymen!" He tried to rise, but his massive bulk slowed him.

"But Sair," Deborah cried, "that's really not necessary." She knelt before him. "*Adonai* has said He will give Sisera into our hands. The battle is already won!"

Sair took her tiny hands into his own. "And I believe that with all of my heart. I do. But that doesn't mean He doesn't expect us to do our part. I've waited for this day for too many years. I will see it through to the end!"

"But you could be killed!"

"And so could every other man out there on that field. Why should I be any different? If I die, then I will die with honor in the service of *Adonai*. What better way can a man ask to meet His judgment?"

"Oh, I don't know. Maybe serving his own neighbors as you have faithfully done for many years now." She bowed her head and confessed to him, "When I was younger, I thought you were a mean old man, but I was wrong. You don't need to do this. You have nothing to prove. You are a good and righteous man, my dear friend."

Sair chuckled and kissed her cheek. "You weren't wrong. You are a true prophetess, and always have been. *Adonai* had to humble me greatly to make me see the error of my ways, and He used you to do it. May His blessings be upon you for many, many years to come. I have to go. I have a son and a godson in that battle. I need to be there for them."

He turned to his wife. "Tell Abel to saddle the camel and the donkey, and please pack up as many provisions as we can carry on them. I'm sure Barak can use all we can bring. And wake everyone up. I'd like to say goodbye. But hurry! We need to leave immediately."

CHAPTER 15

I will draw out to you Sisera, the commander of Jabin's army, with his
chariots and his many troops to the river Kishon, and I will give him into
your hand. Judges 4:7

It took several days for Sair to find Barak. Maybe Abel could have gotten there a bit faster if he had traveled alone, but Sair doubted it. Deborah was certainly right. The land was crawling with enemy troops. Speed wouldn't help if the messenger was dead before he could deliver it.

A man of his bulk couldn't hope for stealth, so he didn't try. He did travel through the back roads, but he dressed in his oldest robes, put his oldest and most ragged and dirty blankets on his animals, and zigzagged from town to town as if he was an itinerant peddler selling a few trinkets and some rather rancid wine. He carried a couple of wineskins of his worst wares for anyone who stopped him to sample. A couple of soldiers tried it and spit it from their mouth. Fortunately, after that, they never bothered to check the rest of his bags.

In each town, he found word of Barak and of Sisera's troops. Although he had stayed at home all this time while Barak did the traveling, Sair was well versed on what had gone on in the day-to-day operations of Barak's troops. He had contacts in every town and tribe in Israel. As he went from town to town, he was also sending out other messengers to rally their troops to come to Barak's aid in Kedesh.

Naturally, Barak wasn't the least bit surprised to hear about Sisera's troops. It wasn't possible to hide that many troops, and Sisera wasn't dumb enough to try. Barak was surprised to see Sair though. When Sair delivered Deborah's message, tears shone on Barak's face.

"Where am I supposed to get ten thousand troops? I don't have half that many. And I can hardly feed the ones I do have! The men are grumbling and complaining more each day. They've seen Sisera's horses and chariots. They've seen his swords and shields. Most of our men are fighting with homemade bows and arrows and spears carved from trees we find on the mountainside. Some of the men fight with rocks and slingshots, or with farm implements like ox goads but they sure can't make them work like Judge Shamgar did. The only decent weapons we have at all are the ones we've taken from Sisera's own troops in our skirmishes with isolated units we've managed to lure into our traps."

As Barak paced back and forth, Sair sat patiently waiting for Barak's anguish to abate. He understood. When he'd gotten that first glimpse of the sea of helmets that gleamed in the sunlight, almost blinding in their intensity, he'd felt the same way. "You're forgetting something, son," he reminded Barak. "This is not your battle. *Adonai* has said He will fight it for you. He will tell you what to do."

Barak shook his head. "No. *Adonai* doesn't speak clearly to me like He speaks to Deborah. Oh, I've had some vague impressions, and most of them have proved right, but I need her by my side letting *Adonai* lead our every move. If the battle is to be won, we must go together. If she won't go, I won't go. You must go back and tell her so."

"I'm not going anywhere," Sair sighed. "Send a swifter messenger, one with both speed and guile, and have him take Abel with him, if you will. My wife made me promise we would send him home immediately. I don't think he wants to go, but I did promise."

Barak chuckled. "I have just the man. I think it's time for Lappidoth the oil vendor to ride again. Most of these are new troops. They don't have any idea what Barak the General looks like. It should be safe enough."

"You can take my camel," Sair offered. "He's a bit cantankerous, but he's sure-footed, and fast enough."

Barak shook his head. "That won't be necessary unless you want to put Abel on it. I think I'll see if I can borrow Jubal's mule. To look at him, you'd think he was about to break down at any moment, but I've seen that mule outrace some of Sisera's finest horses."

Sair laughed. "Abel's donkey is about the same way. I know I shouldn't encourage him, but I've seen Abel take many *shekels* out of other boys' money purses wagering on the animal. To be truthful, I've put a few *shekels* in my own pocket the same way! Besides, two donkeys would draw less attention than a camel does."

Barak called Joshua in and put him in charge of the camp until he returned. He gave instructions to give a double ration to each man for their dinner in celebration to *Adonai* for His assurance that the victory was theirs.

After Joshua had left, Barak and Sair ate a stew Abigail made from the provisions Sair had brought. From the way Barak ate, Sair wondered when the last time he had eaten well was. He had spoken of his men's hunger, but Sair knew him well enough to know that if the men didn't have much, Barak had even less. He ate with gusto.

"Sair, I think the next task is for you to take your camel, go into Kedesh, and work on the recruitment. We need as many men as we can get, as swiftly as possible. You were right. This is *Adonai's* battle, and He has asked for ten thousand men from Zebulun and Naphtali. Begin there, but don't neglect to also ask anyone you see from Reuben's, or Asher's, or Dan's tribes to join us as well. We need all of Israel united together if we're to fight this battle. As an older man, you may be able to travel more freely without raising suspicion from Sisera's troops." He gave Sair his signet ring. "But you may find some opposition by those who think you're trying to lure them into one of Sisera's traps. This will be a sign to them that you come in my name."

Sair beamed. This was the kind of task he could do well. His travels as a wine merchant had taught him how to talk to men about war. It was a subject men loved to talk about. Now was their time to live their talk. He was absolutely sure he could persuade them to do so. It was also nice to think that after all these years, *Adonai* had not forgotten him after all. His age might be of benefit to the cause.

CHAPTER 16

Then Barak said to her, "If you will go with me, then I will go; but if you will not go with me, I will not go." Judges 4:8

"Good morning, my beloved." Barak greeted Deborah as she bent over the old wooden tub soaking her wicks. He couldn't help but be reminded of that day when he had seen her bent over this same tub on the day of Ehud's funeral lament. Was it even possible that was twenty years ago? She still looked so much the same to him. Yes, there were a few wrinkles around her eyes, and she was a bit heavier when she ran into his arms and embraced him. However, her spirit hadn't seemed to age a day. Her eyes still shone with exuberance for life and love for him. Her kisses still tasted sweeter than a honey cake on a hot day. On the other hand, he knew he was weary. So much death and destruction had left a mark on his soul.

"What are you doing here?" she whispered as she nuzzled his neck. "Aren't you supposed to be in a battle with Sisera right about now?"

Barak shook his head. "The men are preparing for the battle. I sent Sair into Kedesh to begin the recruitment. I didn't have even half the troops you asked for at the camp. You don't know the size of Sisera's army. He has more than nine hundred iron chariots and more men and horses than I can count. The men are afraid. I came to get my wife. I need your wisdom to tell me what to do, and I can't wait the time it takes to send messengers back and forth. I know *Adonai* is on our side, but we simply can't do this without you. So, I came to get you. If you will go with me, then I will go, but if you will not go with me, then I will not go."

Deborah pursed her lips, a habit she had when she was about to say something she thought he might not like. He had always found it adorable.

"I will surely go with you; nevertheless, the honor shall not be yours on the journey that you are about to take, for the Lord will sell Sisera into the hands of a woman."

Barak laughed. "Do you still know me so little, wife, as to think I would care whether Sisera was sold into my hands or yours?"

"No. They will not be my hands either. *Adonai* has other plans for Sisera."

"As long as he's no longer able to oppress Israel, so be it." He picked her up as easily as he had twenty years ago. "Those have to soak a while before you can take them out, right? I once remember you telling me you were never too tired to properly greet your husband after a long journey. Does that still hold true?" Perhaps he wasn't as tired as he'd thought either.

Deborah laughed. "Surely it does. We should also stop by the Tabernacle later to offer a sacrifice of thanksgiving for the success of the battle."

"But we haven't won yet."

"Exactly. Our offering shows our confidence that *Adonai* goes ahead of us, and the battle is won not by our hands, but by His alone!"

At the tabernacle, Eli greeted them. "Lappidoth, how good to see you! It has been a long time since I have seen the face of my friends. My dear Deborah, may *Adonai*'s peace be upon you!"

"Thank you Eli." Barak breathed a sigh of relief that Eli hadn't forgotten. "And who is this fine young man?" He rubbed the head of the little long-haired boy half-hiding behind Eli's leg.

"This is Samuel. Won't you properly greet my friends, Samuel?"

The little boy came out and bowed low before them. "Blessed be the Name of *Adonai*, and blessed are you both."

Then he quickly hid back behind Eli.

"So you have another son! Congratulations."

"Thank you. Indeed *Adonai* has entrusted another child to my care, but he is not my son. He is the hope for Israel's future. You may know his mother and father. They are from your town. Elkanah, son of Jeroham, and Hannah.

Deborah spoke up. "Elkanah, the husband of Peninnah?"

Eli coughed. "Yes, I believe that is his first wife's name. So you know her?"

"Yes," Deborah laughed. "I know her. She's rather contentious, but she generally manages to have the law on her side."

"She would." Eli agreed. "Hannah was barren until Samuel was born. Peninnah was very hateful to her. Hannah came here crying out to *Adonai* for a son, and when He granted her request, she made a Nazarite vow. The boy has been dedicated to the Lord since before he was born, and he's been with me since he was weaned. He's so different from how my boys ever were."

"Just be sure to discipline him well so that he stays that way," Barak said.

"I will, and my wife won't stop me this time either. She's seen the results with our sons, and she doesn't wish that for Samuel any more than I do. But truthfully, Samuel doesn't seem to need nearly the discipline my sons needed but lacked. It's as if he has the fire of love for *Adonai* burning brightly within him even at this young age."

Deborah nodded. "I know exactly what you mean. My Halal was always the same way. I never made a Nazarite vow for him although, truthfully, I did think about it, but it was like I didn't need to. His destiny was praise, and he fulfilled it on his own."

"Yes," Eli replied. "I know Halal. He stopped here on his way to the battle also, and he was singing *Adonai*'s praises even as he left here. His spirit is so strong just like Samuel's is. But I worried about him. He seemed to know that trouble was ahead for him, and he feared not for himself, but for you and his wife and daughter."

CHAPTER 17

*There was peace between Jabin the king of Hazor
and the House of Heber the Kenite. Judges 4:17b*

Jael dropped her cooking spoon. Had she heard her husband right? He couldn't possibly be suggesting what it sounded like. "You want me to what?!"

Heber leaned back in his cushions, munching on the roasted leg of lamb Jael had just drawn out of the pot for him. "Don't be so upset about this. It's not that important. Lots of wives do it for their husbands. Why are you making such a big fuss about this?"

She sat at his feet. "Heber, you just asked me to sleep with Sisera, and you think that's not important!"

He continued to munch. "This is good. You should cook this for Sisera. I think he'd like it. Look, it's just that Jabin says that Sisera is depressed. Sisera is upset that his concubine ran away. He really liked this one and, apparently, she looks a lot like you. Like I said before, he may not even come through here on his way back to camp. But if he does, Jabin just wants you to make him feel welcome. He thinks you could comfort Sisera like no one else could, and Jabin wants him calm and focused for the battle."

"But Jewish wives don't sleep with other men. It's called adultery."

"Sure they do. Didn't Abraham and Isaac both give their wives to other men? It's not adultery if your husband tells you to."

"And what a disaster that was in both cases! It's wrong, Heber! It's always been wrong!"

Between bites of lamb, he said, "Besides, you're not really Jewish. We're Kenites. You worship *Adonai* because He was the god of your friend Rachel. But as far as I can see, one god is as good as any other."

"If all you're talking about is your pieces of carved wood and stone, you're absolutely right. One is just as good as any other, because they're all worthless! But *Adonai* isn't like one of your idols. He's real! And He would not approve of your scheme to gain favor with Jabin this way! You don't know what Sisera is capable of. He could kill me. He's done it many times before."

"Don't be ridiculous. Why would he do that? You're a great lover. Everything a man could want. He will be very pleased with you. I guaranteed Jabin of that very thing!"

CHAPTER
18

Then they told Sisera that Barak the son of Abinoam had gone up to Mount Tabor. Judges 4:12

As Sair went through the town, he gathered as many of the men of Kedesh as he could, and he was liberally sharing with them his best wines. That made it much easier for him to get them to talk and speak freely as to where their true sentiments lay. Barak already knew exactly where Sisera's army was; that wasn't the information he was seeking. He wanted to know Sisera's plans.

To his astonishment, he found that many of the men greatly admired Sisera; that they had made him into this mythical god in their own minds, who would be impossible to stop because he could feed an army without food, because he could swim through the water and catch fish in his beard, and he could fell trees with the mere sound of his voice.

His task was going to be much harder than he had thought. He talked with men of Gilead. They shook their heads and said they had too many concerns at home.

He talked to men of Dan. They said they were protecting the seacoast from any invasion from that direction, and couldn't leave their ships.

He talked to men of Asher and got basically the same response.

The men of Reuben were divided. Some wanted to go, many didn't. They were more worried about their own sheepfolds, but even those who wanted to go argued about who would go first, and exactly when and where they would go and wouldn't go. It gave him a headache, just listening to them.

Everywhere he went though, fear was his greatest foe. Like Joshua and Caleb of old, he needed to convince these men that they could defeat a giant, because *Adonai* their God was greater than any earthly giant.

"Don't I know you?" Sair turned at the sound of the squeaky, high-pitched voice of a youngster he had met a few times at Deborah's home.

"Yes. Eliab, isn't it? The blessings of *Adonai* be upon you." He bowed the customary greeting, which Eliab only returned as slightly as was considered acceptable. "What brings you to Kedesh? And looking so fine in your festal robes too. I didn't know your father could afford such finery." He didn't mention that he had seen Joshua only a few days before, and he definitely wasn't wearing silk.

"He isn't my father," Eliab said bitterly. "My father is dead and has been since before I was born. And these aren't festal robes either. They're what I wear every day now. I'm a rich man, someone who matters, not a peasant like Joshua. My grandfather died, and I inherited his wealth from my true father."

As he strutted a bit like a peacock, Sair couldn't help but sigh as he was reminded of his own former attitudes.

"I'm someone to be reckoned with in this town," he repeated. "Anyone can tell you that."

The men with Sair nodded mutely, acknowledging the accuracy, if not the intent, of the message.

"I'm even entertaining Sisera himself this evening," he proudly boasted.

Sair's brows lifted. This was good news indeed. "Oh, really?" He laid his arm around the boy's shoulders and walked away from the men he'd been with. "I've heard so much about the man. I would be greatly pleased to meet him myself."

Eliab glanced back warily. He knew a few of the men Sair had been with, but not well enough to know their politics. "'Well, you are an old friend of my *Ima*'s. It might be good for you to come. If you'd like to be at my home for dinner by sunset, my *Safta* would be pleased to introduce you."

He gazed at Sair's worn robes. "And if you have nothing nicer to wear, my *Safta* will be pleased to provide you with something. I think you're about the same size my *Saba* was."

That evening, as they sat over one of the largest meals Sair had eaten in a long, long while, Sair could see why Sisera was so admired by so many. He was a courteous dinner guest, and he did have a fine deep voice that resonated with his laughter throughout the magnificent house.

Eliab welcomed Sisera with all the usual greetings and blessings, although Sair noted he never kissed Sisera's cheek in the customary manner. But he did offer him a towel as the servant washed his feet, and he waited to usher him into the front room where a lavish meal had already been set out for the men. Naturally, the wine flowed liberally, and Sair was pleased to discover that it was his own from one of his best years.

At first, Eliab seemed to dance around with the exuberance Sair remembered from when he was smaller. But as the evening wore on, he became quieter and quieter. When Sisera's eyes glistened with the effects of his wine, Sair leaned close.

"I've seen your troops in the valley. What a fine army you have. The golden gleam of their many helmets almost blinded me as I came through there. Barak's ragtag scraps should be no problem for you at all."

Sisera roared with laughter. "If we could find the dogs, they'd be done for by morning, and we'd all be celebrating a great day for your people by tomorrow night. Jabin is a great king. He rewards his servants well." He winked at Sair, and whispered, "Israel would prosper greatly under his leadership, and so would anyone who aided in Jabin's cause. My men march proudly in the daylight. Barak and his men hide like dogs in the darkness of the mountains and only come out when the moon is in their favor."

Sair rubbed his mouth as if he was considering Sisera's offer. He didn't want to appear too eager. "Well, I was talking with some men this afternoon, and I heard one of them say that Barak was headed to Mt. Tabor."

"Mt. Tabor? Isn't that down near the Kishon River?" Sisera's eyes glistened even more. "Are you absolutely sure about that?"

Sair shrugged. "As sure as I can be. I'd never met the man before, but he was recruiting some others to join Barak so I assume he knew what he was talking about. I try to stay out of politics myself. It isn't good for the wine business to take sides. This is truly some of my best wine. Won't you join me for another cup?"

About that time, Eliab's *Safta* brought a young female servant into the room with her. Sair watched Eliab's jaw drop open and his eyes spark. "General Sisera," she said, "I've brought you a young maiden to be your companion for the night. I'm sure she will warm your bed in a manner quite pleasing to you."

Sisera gazed at the girl intently for a moment as if trying to decide what to do next, but he shook his head. "Thank you for the kind offer. But I need to get back to my troops immediately. I must go now!"

After Sisera left, Eliab was irate. He paced back and forth, shaking his finger at Sair. "Are you drunk, or are you mad?" he shouted. "You have just betrayed to the enemy one of the greatest men our land has ever known! And *Safta*, how could you offer up a virgin of Israel as a sacrifice to Sisera's insane lust? I've heard what he does to women who don't please him, and even worse, what he does to those who do! What has happened to our country? Is Israel no longer the land of *Adonai*? Are we no longer His servants? We don't betray our friends! We don't give up our women! A little extra food and some silken robes just aren't worth it!"

With that, he tore off the festal robe and stood there in nothing but his tunic, which he also ripped down the middle like his best friend had died.

Sair roared with a laughter that would have easily rivaled Sisera's. "Praise be to *Adonai*! You have at last come to your senses! No, I am neither drunk nor mad. It would take far more wine than I've drunk tonight to make me lose my head. I've been a wine merchant since I was a scrap of a boy far younger than you are, or at least were until only a few moments ago."

He stood and clapped Eliab on the back. "*Adonai* be praised, the boy is now a man! And the only one I betrayed here tonight was Sisera, and perhaps your hospitality. That was the message meant to be given to him. I had no idea I'd be able to deliver it personally though. Thank you for that opportunity. Now, since you have finally decided whose side you're on, would you care to join me? I have to get back to Barak and let him know the jackal is headed for the henhouse." He glanced at Eliab's *Safta*. "And I hate to say it, but perhaps we need to take her with us. I'm afraid she might get her message delivered before we could deliver ours."

The old woman grinned. "That won't be necessary. My grandson has been struggling in his loyalties since the day he got here. I think he thought that if he admitted that he loved Joshua, he would be somehow disloyal to my son, Jacob. Nothing could be further from the truth. Joshua is a wonderful man. He has kept us updated on Eliab his whole life. I only wish my husband's health had allowed us to travel to see Eliab more often."

She turned slightly toward Eliab, and pushed the young girl forward toward him, but still spoke more to Sair. "This is the same maiden I've been pushing on Eliab since that first day. She's been a devoted friend to me all her life, and would do anything for me. I had hoped Eliab might then claim her as his wife. As a house-born slave, it's her only real chance. I knew he was greatly attracted to her, but because he does love *Adonai* deep in his heart, he was able to resist the temptation. I thought by offering her to Sisera tonight, I might provoke him to see the truth. Naturally, I knew that she isn't at all Sisera's type. He likes them skinny and boyish. She has far too many curves."

She clapped her hands in delight. "Did you see Sisera's face when you mentioned Mt. Tabor? It's rumored that his latest concubine escaped back to her home on the Kishon River. I'll wager he's going that way in hopes of meeting up with her as much as to battle Barak! Praise be to *Adonai*, it has all worked together."

She took Eliab's hand and placed the young girl's in it. "I'll admit, my concern was far more for Eliab than Sisera though. I could see it in Eliab's face when we walked through the door. He knew what I was going to do, and he was furious! He knows now who he is, and he's a faithful son of Israel!"

She bent to begin picking up bowls with scraps of food left scattered around the room. "With the blessings of the house of Micah ben Caleb, go! Both of you! Quickly! I promise you there will be no message sent from this house unless it's sent by my servants to Barak's camp when they take him their next packages of provisions. They might have starved to death by now, were it not for my husband's steward. He's been smuggling provisions to them without getting caught for years now. We send as much as we can, but the army grows larger and larger, and even we can't afford to feed them all as well as we'd like. And too much at one time would likely be intercepted by Sisera. My husband was one of Barak's first supporters. When he saved Eliab's life before he was born, Barak gave us the greatest gift we have ever received other than his father. Micah took his wealth for granted but it never owned him like it owned Jacob, and I was afraid it was going to do with Eliab."

Eliab hooted with laughter as he grabbed up his robe and the young maiden helped him put it back on. "*Safta*, you're the wisest woman I know. I did like her. I did want her, but not as a concubine. I claim her as my wife right now. Sair is my witness. Don't give her to anyone else. We can have the wedding ceremony the moment I return. And I want it to be the greatest wedding this town has seen. A virgin of Israel deserves nothing less!"

CHAPTER 19

The torrent of Kishon swept them away, the ancient torrent, the torrent Kishon. O my soul, march on with strength. Judges 5:21

Lilith shivered with the cold and wrapped Athtor's cloak tighter around her. Winter on the Kishon River wasn't generally pleasant weather anyway, and a storm was brewing that mirrored her mood. The money Athtor had given her was gone, stolen by the two men Athtor had hired to take her down the river. At least she had gotten this far, and the men hadn't killed her, only beaten her and taken off with the money. That wasn't true either. She shuddered to think what else they had done to her, but what did it really matter? That would probably be her profession from now on anyway. To fight the despair that was rapidly enveloping her, she hugged her belly and began to talk to the baby.

"It's going to be fine, Torah. Your *Safta* said you were going to study the Torah in Jerusalem. So in the Name of *Adonai*, I'm going to claim that as your destiny. We're going to make it home safely, and somehow I'm going to raise you to be a fine young man of the law. *Adonai*'s protection is upon you now, and He will find a way to make it happen." She began to sing an old song her *Ima* had sung to her as a baby.

Moses' Ima put him in a basket, sailed him down the Nile, sailed him down the Nile. Covered it over with tar and pitch, and sailed him down the Nile, sailed him down the Nile. To save her baby, she sailed him down the Nile, sailed him down the Nile. To the arms of a princess, she sailed him down the Nile, sailed him down the Nile.

The song had a calming effect on her, much like it had when she was little. Perhaps her *Ima* would remember that sometimes women had to do hard things, like giving their own children away to keep them safe. She shook her head. No, *Ima* would never understand. She would say it would have been better for Lilith to kill herself than to willingly submit to Sisera's embrace. She hugged her belly again. Was it so wrong not to regret having this baby in her womb? She had screamed plenty when she had been taken from her home, but what good would it have done to scream in Sisera's palace? All it would have done is gotten her killed.

And she had come to love him. In his own way, maybe he loved her too. He'd been willing to send his own mother away. The woman had a strange hold on him that Lilith didn't quite understand, but certainly wasn't natural for a man his age. How had Athtor known exactly how to please Sisera? Had she spied on him with other women? Had she spied on him with her? Or...

A twig broke nearby. Someone was coming! She hid.

As they neared the riverbank, Halal gestured to his companions. "I tell you I heard a woman's voice singing. It was a song my *Ima* used to sing to me all the time. I know I didn't imagine it. It was coming from over here."

Jubal hushed Halal. "I believe you. Just be quiet. It could still be a trap."

Jubal stared at Nathan. "I still don't know how I let you two talk me into going on this crazy mission of mythical mercy. There is simply no way we're going to find Sisera's concubine out here in the middle of nowhere. If there even was such a person, she's probably either dead or in another country far away from here by now. Just because she supposedly came from somewhere around the Kishon River doesn't mean she'd ever come back here. She'd know that if she did, her own parents might kill her."

Nathan shook his head. "No, she's not dead. I told you, *Adonai* told me to come here. He said she'd be here, and I was to marry her and take her to Jerusalem with me when all of this is over."

Lilith stepped out from her hiding place. Tears streamed from her eyes. "Is that true? *Adonai* really sent you for me?"

He nodded. Her beauty took his breath away. This was the woman *Adonai* had chosen to be his bride?

"You know that I bear Sisera's child? Why would *Adonai* still care for me after what I have done?"

Nathan shrugged. "*Adonai* told me about the child. It is written that he will study Torah in Jerusalem. *Adonai*'s children have often failed Him. It doesn't make Him love them less, but He does discipline them to cause them to turn back to Him. That's why our land has suffered so for years now. Who am I to question the ways of *Adonai*?"

"What else did He tell you? Does He speak to you often?"

"Often enough," he admitted. "He says I am to be a prophet to kings, but first I am to faithfully teach our sons and many others His ways."

"All right, all right." Jubal interrupted. "I'd never have believed it possible, but we've accomplished what we came here to do. Can we please get out of here now? We need to get back to camp. I was supposed to be back two days ago. The General is going to think we've all been killed or captured."

As he spoke, the rains began to come down in a great torrent and soaked them through. They ran for the horses. Lightning streaked across the sky and fierce thunder cracked. The horses reared up and took off.

"Now what are we to do?" Jubal threw his hands in the air. "Did *Adonai* tell you about this too, Nathan? If so, you should have warned me!"

"No," Nathan shouted over the noise of the storm. "He didn't tell me this."

"We need to get to higher ground," Lilith cried. "It's way too dangerous down here by the riverbank."

"Halal? Where's Halal?" Jubal called out.

"He was right behind us!" Nathan cried. "Halal, where are you?"

As the rain continued to beat on them relentlessly, they all began to yell and scream as they continued to search for their friend.

CHAPTER 20

Deborah said to Barak, "Arise! For this is the day in which the Lord has given Sisera into your hands." Judges 4:14a

When they had entered the camp and found that Halal and Nathan had gone out on patrol with Jubal and had not returned when they were due back, Deborah's worst fears were confirmed. *Adonai* had taken another child from her. She cried out to Him all night long, but He was silent, and soon Deborah was silent too. She didn't speak at all for three days.

Abigail tried to minister to her needs and to comfort her, but Deborah was beyond comfort at the time. She ate and drank nothing at all. They had continued to move toward Mt. Tabor, of course, and Deborah moved right along with them, but without a word from Deborah, no one was certain what they would do when they got there. Thanks to all of Sair's efforts, they did have their ten thousand men now, but what was that against Sisera's army?

When Jubal and Nathan finally reappeared, bringing with them a beautiful but bedraggled young woman, Barak had immediately summoned them and demanded an accounting. Nathan explained everything as best he could, telling Barak who Lilith was and how *Adonai* had spoken to him telling him where to find her, and how he and Halal had convinced Jubal that they had to go to get her.

Then Nathan finally said, "We don't know what happened to him, sir. He was right behind us, but it was raining so hard, and there were so many streaks of lightening and cracks of thunder, it frightened the horses, and they took off, and we took off after them, but when we turned around, Halal wasn't with us anymore. There weren't any footprints on the riverbank, but it was raining so hard, there couldn't be anyway. We searched and searched, but we never found any sign of him. We even went down to Meroz, and tried to organize a search party to go out and help us look for him, but they refused. Then, when we told them Sisera was headed this way, they said it was none of their business, and we needed to get out of town before we brought his army down on them. They threw rocks at us to make us leave. "

Barak buried his face in his hands. Halal had always been a bit clumsy. It would have been so easy for him to lose his footing on a slippery riverbank. But why hadn't any of them heard him cry out? Maybe he did, but no one could hear him over the crash of the thunder. It was the only thing that made any sense.

But why would *Adonai* send them to a slippery riverbank in the first place to save a girl who had willingly given herself to the enemy? Why would He trade their son, who was so good and pure, for her? Why?

At dawn the next morning, Deborah arose, washed, and put on clean garments. Then she went in to waken Barak. "Arise! For this is the day in which the Lord has given Sisera into your hands; behold, the Lord has gone out before you."

Then, amazingly, he thought he heard her singing. Surely he must be mistaken. No, he heard it again.

Barak stared at her.

CHAPTER
21

The Lord routed Sisera and all his chariots and all his army with the edge of the sword before Barak; and Sisera alighted from his chariot and fled away on foot. Judges 4:15

As he brought his troops down to the same riverbank where Halal had disappeared and Sisera's men were now encamped, Barak wondered if *Adonai* could have possibly picked a worse day to do battle. The torrents of rain that had apparently washed away his only son had started up again and continued to pour down as lightning flashed and thunder crashed like a musical accompaniment to the noise of the battle. His men were drenched and so was he.

Further back from the fighting, up on the hillside, Deborah sat on her horse seemingly oblivious to the weather as she raised her hands toward heaven and prayed. Faithful Abigail, a righteous widow of the tribe of Benjamin, stayed right beside her, and whenever one of his men was injured, other men would attempt to take him up to Abigail as quickly as possible. By now, she tore her own garments to make bandages to make splints or tie wounds too deep to bandage any other way. He tried to keep an eye on the safety of the women, but his blade was too busy for him to think much about the weather or to pray much either. He saw that some of the other kings of smaller provinces of northern Canaan had also joined Sisera's troops.

Only the princes of Issachar had joined his own ranks. He had gotten word, though, that one of Joshua's lieutenants had led the tribe of Ephraim to band together to cut off the king of Amalek from joining the battle from the south.

As the morning wore on, he saw the complete perfection of *Adonai*'s plans. The heavy iron chariots quickly became mired in the marshy lowlands by the riverbank. No matter how hard the riders tried to whip the horses into moving, the chariots wouldn't budge. They were useless. Worse than useless really, because the horses had to be disengaged from them to have any chance of escape, and the weight of the chariot kept pulling the horse backward as he fought against the ropes.

Many of Sisera's men were killed by their own horses' hooves, and the fallen men's weapons were easy pickings for Barak's troops. Now armed with Sisera's own swords and shields, Barak's men were more than equal to the task of taking down the frightened and disoriented enemy troops.

The bravery of Barak's troops astonished even him. Their fear was gone. It was as if they could sense that Sisera was now the one who needed to be afraid. Even to the point of certain death, they rushed into whole clusters of Sisera's men, and took out a dozen men before themselves falling to a blade. Aholiab was just such a one. This former thief, but even better spy, a brave tribesman of Zebulun, gladly gave up his own life for the sake of Israel. But, among others, he took two of the kings of Canaan down with him.

Many of Sisera's men did disappear over the side of the riverbank as they fought too near the edge, or sought the river as a path to escape, and Barak did hear their screams. The river branched to a side stream near Megiddo. It was full of quicksand.

As they ran to escape the torrent of the river, some ran right into the sand. Horses broke their legs as they too tried to get away from the deadly mire. Still, the rain didn't cease. In fact, it had turned to large hailstones, some the size of gold nuggets, and in the flashes of lightening, Barak saw stars hurled from heaven, as if *Adonai* Himself had now joined the battle.

Sisera's men saw them too. Panic ensued as huge craters formed on the field when the large rocks hit the earth with such force that they split the ground and disappeared into the earth right where, moments before, chariots and horses had been. That frightened Sisera's men far more than Barak's troops had. Even they couldn't fight against *Adonai*, and they knew it!

It was right after one of these hit that Barak saw Sisera get out of his own chariot and run with all his might. Barak tried to go after him, but there were so many men abandoning their chariots and running for their lives. And many of them were running right into the blades of Israel's army. He soon lost sight of Sisera. There were too many men between them, and all he could do was keep fighting.

Suddenly, he heard Abigail scream. He looked up. A red-headed man and another man were headed toward her with swords drawn.

"You killed my brother," the dark-haired man screamed. "Now you'll pay."

There was no way Barak could get there first. But he needn't have worried. Joshua and Jubal had it covered. The attacking men never even made it halfway up the hill. Perhaps they had been so intent on Abigail they hadn't even noticed the sure-footed mules coming up behind them.

"This man is an Israelite," Joshua cried when he pulled out his blade. "Why is he fighting against us?"

"Why do evil men do evil things?" Abigail replied. "My step-son was an evil man. He had no love for *Adonai*. So evil had free reign in his life." She pointed at the dead red-headed man. "That is the man Joram hired to rape me."

CHAPTER 22

*But Barak pursued the chariots and the army as far as Harosheth-hagoyim,
and all the army of Sisera fell by the sword; not even one was left.*
Judges 4:16

As some of the chariot riders around the fringes of the field that had not been so deeply mired worked together, they were able to get their chariots loose. Seeing the large holes in the ground, and all the dead horses and riders, as well as that their own General had fled, they too threw down their excess armor and decided to make a run for it. Barak ordered his men to forget the plunder and give chase. Perhaps they could lead him to Sisera. He looked over at Deborah. She hadn't moved. Her arms were still held high, just as Moses had held his up when Israel fought against the first Amalek. But the battle was over now.

He rode up to her. "Beloved, it's over," he whispered. "Sisera has run away. I'm going after him."

She smiled at him and lowered her arms for Barak to lift her off the horse. "Take your time. There's no hurry. You will not find him alive. But tell your men to have no mercy. Not one of his troops must be left alive. *Adonai* has decreed it."

"Did you see how He hurled stars from heaven? From their courses, they fought against Sisera, and his men were so terrified, they fought each other in their hurry to flee."

She nodded. "I saw it all. From the beginning, Sisera's troops had no hope. Who can begin to fight against *Adonai*? We're so foolish to try. Yet we do. All we can say is 'Blessed are You, King of the Universe. You give and take away. Blessed be the Name of *Adonai*.'"

She had gone from talking about Sisera to herself. She had accepted the loss of another child as the will of *Adonai*. He wasn't so sure he did. Why had no one heard a scream? Even above all the noise of the battle, he'd heard plenty of screams today.

CHAPTER 23

Jael went out to meet Sisera, and said to him, "Turn aside, my master, turn aside to me! Do not be afraid." Judges 4:18a

The group of large, black, goatskin tents under the oak tree was a welcome sight. He must be near Zaanannim. He was saved. This was the Kenite camp. The Kenites were allies of Jabin's and he would find shelter and safety here for sure.

"Pssst, Sisera, over here!" Jael swiveled her hips and gestured for him to come to Heber's tent. "Turn aside, my master, turn aside to me. Don't be afraid." She held up the tent flap. "Please come in and be comfortable."

Sisera sighed. He was exhausted. For a moment, when he first saw her, he thought it was Lilith, and his heart pounded for joy. Of course, by the time he reached Heber's tent, he could see that it wasn't Lilith, only Jael, the wife of Heber. He'd met her before, but hadn't realized the strong resemblance to Lilith. She had the same long, dark hair and the same boyish figure and that same scent of jasmine and myrrh that drove him wild with desire.

He expected to see Heber when he entered the tent, but he wasn't anywhere around. She led him to her side of the tent. He'd been on Heber's side many times before, but never here. Women didn't bring men to their chambers. Even when Heber wanted his wife, she would go to him, not the other way. The room was dimly lit, but had many thick, soft, silken cushions. It smelled just like Jael did.

Now that he was inside, Jael seemed a bit more nervous and reserved. "I hope the battle went well for you," she whispered.

She didn't wait for an answer, which was good, because he didn't care to give one.

"You're soaked through. Get under this rug and get warm. You must be so tired. Here, let me wash your feet for you." As she began to wash and rub his feet with fragrant oils, he began to relax and she seemed to calm down too.

"Please give me a little water to drink," he croaked, the rasp in his voice caused by his dry, dusty, throat. "I'm so thirsty."

She arose and went into the back of the tent. Bringing him a skin of milk, she said, "Here, this is better. I can see how tired you are. Milk always helps me to sleep like my baby girl."

She also brought him a carved wooden bowl of curds and other delicacies to ease the hunger that he hadn't realized he felt until the aroma of her offerings tempted him. As he ate, and drank the milk, she began to massage his neck and shoulders. He did indeed begin to relax somewhat, but he also began to feel that same urge he always felt when he was with Lilith. So he pulled Jael around and down. As he did, an alabaster comb fell from her hair and she landed on it, breaking it with a loud snap.

"No, you broke my comb," she cried, struggling to get up.

"It's of no importance," he growled. "I'll get you another later." His lust was already past caring about such a trivial thing as a comb. He pushed her back down and had his way with her. She only cried out for a moment before he smothered her cries with his lips, and soon her cries were mingled with the excitement of a lust that nearly matched his own.

Of course, he readily admitted that he was a man with a huge sexual appetite, and once didn't even begin to satisfy him. When, at last, his appetite had been completely sated, he needed to sleep.

He caressed her arm. "Jabin will be expecting a report from me of the day's events. I must go, but I've got to get some sleep before I can travel any further. Stand in the doorway of the tent, and watch for me. If anyone comes and inquires of you if anyone is here, tell them no."

Jael pulled her robe around her. "Certainly, Master," she bowed low before him. She began to rub and nuzzle his neck again. "Yes, you must rest now. It's been a hard day. You're safe here."

She covered him with the rug again. "And when you talk with your king, you can tell Jabin that the hospitality of Heber the Kenite is everything he desired it to be."

CHAPTER 24

She reached out her hand for the tent peg, and her right hand for the workmen's hammer. Judges 5:26

At last, Sisera was fast asleep. He would sleep soundly. His deep snores gave proof of that. She had ground up some poppies and put them in the milk, something her mother had done when anyone was sick and needed to sleep. Of course, she had used twice as many as her mother had. She had no idea how he had managed to still have so much energy after drinking the milk. He had called her Lillith twice. It almost made her feel sorry for him. Almost.

As she watched him sleep, Jael knew what she had to do. For Israel. For Rachel. She picked up her broken alabaster comb and went to the back of the tent. From the workbasket, she fetched the largest workmen's hammer she could find and picked out the longest iron tent peg Heber had. It was almost two spans long, and about the size of the iron scythe that had pierced Rachel's head; the iron scythes that continued to gore the army of Israel.

She covered his face with the rug. In spite of what he had just done to her, she could not look at him and strike the blow that would kill him. With her left hand, she held the tent peg to the rug right at his temple. And with her right hand, she swung with all her might. Sisera's huge body only jerked once as the peg pierced his temple. She continued to swing the hammer until his head was shattered and smashed, just as Rachel's had been by his black stallion.

She returned to the back of the tent, poured water and bathed herself several times. Although the blood was easily removed, somehow she couldn't seem to rid herself of the stink of the day's filth.

Afterwards, she went and sat outside and waited. Finally, she saw Barak in the distance. She went out to meet him. "Come with me," she beckoned him with a wave. "I'll show you whom you're seeking."

Barak followed Jael into the tent. He gasped when she pulled back the rug, and he stared at the sight of Sisera lying dead with the tent peg in his temple. Even though Deborah had warned him to expect it, the sight was rather sickening. He'd seen many men die in battle. That was expected. But Sisera face seemed peaceful. He was naked, and he might have been merely asleep in an elaborate silk-cushioned bed except that a tent peg protruded from his smashed head. *Adonai*'s vengeance could seem cruel.

Yet it was a great day for Israel. The mighty, invincible Sisera was dead. Now all he had to do was get Jabin.

CHAPTER 25

Out of the window she looked and lamented, the mother of Sisera through the lattice, "Why does his chariot delay in coming? Why do the hoofbeats of his chariots tarry?" Judges 5:28

Athtor stared out of the window miserably. All day and into the night she stared. "Why does his chariot delay," she demanded of her servants. "Go, and listen in the village to see if anyone has had any word."

"We've done that several times." The wise young princess who tried to reassure her was one of Jabin's daughters who had been sent into her care as a possible bride for Sisera when he delivered a victory. "And we've left word that we're to be notified immediately if anyone hears anything. But so far, nothing. Perhaps they're finding and dividing the spoils. A maiden or two for every warrior, and to Sisera a fine garment of dyed linen with double embroidery on the yoke of the neck."

Still, Athtor waited and paced. And when she finally got the word, she plunged a dagger into her own chest.

CHAPTER 26

Thus let all Your enemies perish, O Lord; But let those who love Him be like the rising of the sun in its might. Judges 5:31a

Sisera's army was defeated. It was simply a matter of chasing down every last one of them. The last was Jabin himself. He had gone into hiding, and had hidden himself well. But, at last, the deed was done. Israel was free. As Barak's army amassed one last time, Deborah began to sing, and Barak soon joined in:

The leaders led in Israel,
The people volunteered,
Bless the Lord!

Hear, O kings; give ear, O rulers!
I — to the Lord, I will sing,
I will sing praise to the Lord,
The God of Israel.

Their song continued, with Deborah singing some parts alone, Barak others, and often them singing together in praise of their beloved *Adonai*. He had truly blessed them. For the first time in twenty years, they were free from the oppression of a wicked king. More importantly, they were united in a spirit of oneness in their service to the Lord their God. As they recounted His mighty deed in sending the hailstones and hurling the stars down from the heavens to destroy the iron chariots, the people began to cheer with a great voice that echoed across the valley. They sang:

The torrent of Kishon swept them away,
The ancient torrent, the torrent Kishon,
O my soul, march on with strength.

Tears flowed freely down Deborah's cheeks as she sang, but she never stopped. A smile slowly spread across Barak's face, because he saw what she hadn't yet. Coming toward them, but still pretty far away, were Jubal and Nathan, and between them, with his arms raised in victory, and his voice raised to join their song, was his only son, Halal.

Let those who love Him
be like the rising of the sun
in its might.
I will sing praise to the Lord,
The God of Israel.

Hallelujah!

THANK YOU!

I hope you enjoyed *Woman of Light*! I need to ask you a favor. Would you help others enjoy this book too?

Recommend it. Please help other readers find this book by recommending it to friends in person and on social media.

Review it. Reviews can be tough to come by these days. You, the reader, have the power to make or break a book. Loved it, hated it – I'd just enjoy your feedback. Please tell other readers what you thought about this book by reviewing it at Amazon. My goal is to have 100 honest reviews on Amazon. Will you help me reach that goal?

And I'd love for you to connect with me on Facebook: facebook.com/Teresa-Pollard-327613814044009

Thank you so much for reading *Woman of Light* and for spending time with me.

In gratitude,
Teresa Pollard

Discussion Questions

Book One

Chapter 1
1. Is there anything you've felt called to do, but circumstances held you back? What can you do about it?
2. What is the significance of Deborah's name ("little bee")? What does your name mean? How does it relate to your life?

Chapter 2
1. In times of mourning, what has God used most often to comfort you?
2. When you picture heaven, what most often comes to mind? Do you think this is an accurate picture according to scripture? (Revelation 21)

Chapter 3
1. Why do you think people tend to see wealth as a sign of God's blessing? Is it a true sign? Why or why not? (Deuteronomy 8:18, Matthew 13:22)
2. Why do our blessings or curses on others matter? (Genesis 12:3, Romans 12:4)

Chapter 4
1. What is the most impressive place you've ever visited? How did it make you feel?
2. Has God ever told you to do something unexpected? How did you react?

Chapter 5
1. What is your greatest fear? How can we appropriate God's power to overcome our deepest fears? (Isaiah 41:10, Matthew 10:29-30)

2. How would you explain death to a small child?

Chapter 6
1. Describe your relationship with your mother-in-law. How might you go about improving the relationship? (If you don't have a mother-in-law or already have a great relationship, think of another difficult person in your life and apply the question to them.)
2. Have you ever become involved in a dispute between your child and another child? Did you do well? If no, how might you have handled things differently?

Chapter 7
1. Has God ever used something really bad to bring about something really good in your life? How does Romans 8:28 relate to that scenario?
2. Why are we so easily susceptible to judging by appearances? How can we change that? (1 Samuel 16:7)

Chapter 8
1. Have you ever had a firmly rooted belief that turned out to be wrong? How did you come to see the truth? How can we open ourselves to seeing truth without falling for cleverly disguised fallacy? (John 8:31-32)
2. Have you ever personally experienced a miracle that couldn't be explained as anything other than the power of God? How did you react? Why is it so important for us to share those experiences with others?

Chapter 9
1. Have you ever narrowly escaped death? How did you react? Why do you think even most Christians fear death?

2. Can you think of any instances where it's possible you may have entertained an angel unaware? Are angels still at work in our world today? What is their job?
3. Can you think of a time when you did something completely unexpected or out of character for you, but it turned out to be exactly what someone else needed at the time?
4. What is the power of praise? How does it help us heal?

Chapter 10
1. Can you think of a time when no action turned out to be just as bad as a wrong action? Why does the Bible warn us about fence-sitting? Are there any areas of your life where you need to get off the fence? (Revelation 3: 15-16)
2. Has someone ever twisted your words around to make them say something entirely different? How did that make you feel? How do people sometimes twist God's words around? How does that make God feel? (Revelation 22:18-19)

Chapter 11
1. Have you ever had to just start over? How did you do it? What were the results?

Chapter 12
1. How can a change of attitude turn a trial into a triumph? Why should Christians be intentional, not just random, in their acts of kindness? (James 1:22)
2. How is the miracle of birth a picture of salvation? (John 3:3-6)
3. Do you know how much God loves you? Have you asked Him to save you? If not, please take the time to do so right now. It's as easy as ABC. A-admit you're a sinner (Romans 3:23). B-believe that Jesus is God's Son, and that He came to live a perfect life and die to pay the penalty for your sins (John 3:16), and C-commit your life to Him (Romans 6:23). Now praise Him for your salvation because it's your gift for the taking.

Chapter 13
1. How is circumcision a picture of God's covenant with Israel? How is it a picture of salvation? (Genesis 17:10, Colossians 2:11)
2. How is it possible for old adversaries to become good friends? How can we seek opportunities to make that happen?

Chapter 14
1. How can we find the perfect balance between love and discipline? Are boys harder to discipline than girls or just different?
2. Why does it seem that some people are just pure evil in spite of their parents' best efforts?

Chapter 16
1. Have you ever almost given up hope for something, when all of a sudden, God told you to give it one more try, and He brought it to pass? Why does God seem to sometimes wait until the very last second to act? (Isaiah 40:31, Romans 5:3-5)

Chapter 17
1. How is it possible to learn to love a child of rape? Was there anything Chesed could have done differently in the story?

Chapter 18
1. How do you define sin? Why does God hate sin so much? What are sin's consequences? (1 John 3:4-9, Romans 3:23,6:23)

Chapter 19
1. Is there a time in your life that, looking back, seems a blur? How is this the body's way of shielding us from pain? How can this be a good thing? How can it be bad?
2. What is survivor's guilt? How can we best deal with it?

Chapter 20
1. How did Sair give Barak sound advice? Why should we seek the advice of godly counselors — or should we? (Proverbs 11:14, 19:20)
2. Why would Barak need separate identities?

Chapter 21
1. In this age of information overload, what safety precautions or self-defense techniques might Christians need to use to be prepared.
2. Deborah says, "One plus *Adonai* will always be enough." Explain. (Matthew 10:28-29, Philippians 4:13)

Chapter 22
1. What New Testament case is this reminiscent of? What are the similarities? What are the differences? Why do you think Jesus handled His case differently? Is this a valid defense?

Chapter 24
1. When can love become destructive? How can we avoid destructive relationships?

Chapter 25
1. When we do make a mistake, what should be our next move? Did Deborah make a mistake here?

Chapter 26
1. How is prayer a powerful tool that Christians often tend to use as a last resort instead of a first response? How can we change that attitude? (Matthew 21:22. Philippians 4:6)
2. How can we learn to "see beyond our eyes?" (Proverbs 2:3-5, 3:5-6, 4:18)

Book Two

Chapter 1
1. Why is giving thanks more profitable than grumbling? If we know this is true, why do we persist in grumbling? (Psalm 92:1, Philippians 2:14)
2. Why would Barak take his men's punishment? Why didn't he just dismiss the charges? What was the effect? Do you think this is realistic? Why or why not?

Chapter 2
1. How can we make ourselves more conscious of the power our words have? How can we use them more wisely? (Psalm 19:14, Ephesians 4:29)

Chapter 3
1. How is Athtor's attitude that it's perfectly permissible to continue to sin as long as we then confess and make a "suitable sacrifice" the attitude of some "Christians" today? Why is this a fallacy? (Romans 6:11-15, 12:1-2)

Chapter 4
1. What hidden gifts or talents do you have that could be used for God's kingdom? How might you go about putting them to use?

Chapter 5
1. How is peacemaking different from compromise? How can we do the former without the latter, or can we? (Matthew 5:9, Titus 3:1-5)

Chapter 6
1. Why do you think women should or should not be in combat?

Chapter 7
1. Why do you think abortion is or isn't murder? When does life begin? (Psalm 139:13, Luke 1:41)

Chapter 8
1. Who is the "Angel of the Lord" in the Old Testament? What is your image of Him like?
2. Have you ever felt called to do something, but the Lord led you through it one baby step at a time with no real vision of the future? What did you do?

Chapter 9
1. Why did God give the *Sabbath*? How can Christians still honor the "*Sabbath*" considering many employers are now requiring them to work on Sunday? (Exodus 20:8-10)
2. Do you feel that church attendance is a privilege or a duty—or not really necessary at all? Is your attitude scriptural? (Psalm 100, Hebrews 10:25)

Chapter 10
1. How can family secrets be a tool for Satan's use? How can we avoid that trap? (John 8:32, Ephesians 4:14-16)
2. Can you remember a particular point in your life when you had to decide for yourself who you wanted to be?

Chapter 12
1. Has anyone ever made a prophecy about your life? How did it affect you? How is prophecy different from fortunetelling? (1 Corinthians 14:4, 2 Peter 1:21)
2. How would you describe the Sisera of this novel? Does he have any good characteristics? What are his fatal flaws?

Chapter 13
1. Does God still speak to people in visions? Why or why not? (Joel 2:28, Acts 2:17, 2 Timothy 4:14-16, 1 Thessalonians 5:20-21, Hebrews 1:1-2)

Chapter 14
1. What is your place of service for the kingdom? How has God changed you to fit you for that service?

Chapter 15
1. What "liabilities" do you have, and how do you think God could turn them into assets?

Chapter 16
1. Why did Barak want Deborah with him? What was her reaction? Did Barak lack faith in God or himself? What's the difference? How can we have confidence without succumbing to pride? (Proverbs 3:26)

Chapter 17
1. How did Heber use Scripture to justify evil? How do some people do that today?

Chapter 18
1. What are the "giants" in your life? How can you prepare yourself to face them? (2 Timothy 2:15)
2. Rather like the prodigal son, Eliab "comes to his senses." Why? Have you ever felt distant from God (even though maybe you never left a church pew)? What did God use to bring you back?

Chapter 19
1. Why would God sacrifice a "good" person to save an "evil" one? Or would He? (Matthew 9:12, 18:11)

Chapter 20
1. What is the symbolism of three days? (Matthew 12: 38-40)
2. What is the purpose of fasting? (Esther 4:16, Matthew 9:21)

Chapter 22
1. Why do we sometimes fight against God? What is the inevitable outcome?

Chapter 23
1. The story of Jael and Sisera is really a tale of a gruesome murder, isn't it? Why do you think the Bible doesn't condemn Jael? Why are her actions NOT an acceptable behavior for a Christian? (Matthew 5:43-48,26:52, Hebrews 4:12)

Chapter 26
1. What is your favorite song of praise? Can you sing it to Him right now? "Hallelujah!"

Acknowledgements

I would like to "sing" my heartfelt praise to my Lord and Savior, Jesus Christ, for His marvelous sacrifice as my Redeemer, thereby gifting me with a glorious salvation, and thank Him for His amazing "love letter," the Bible which continuously reminds me of His great love and promises.

I'd also like to thank my family and friends, especially Candi and Krystal, for being my partners in "song." There were so many times in the last few years when Krystal and I marched up a mountainside loudly singing songs and hymns of praise just to get to a waterfall at the top. Those were times for me of great spiritual healing. Candi can't actually sing much nowadays, but I still remember her amazingly deep voice from when she was younger. That was the voice I remembered as I wrote the story of Deborah.

A special thank you to my Writers of Light group from Hebron Baptist Church in Dacula, GA, for all their help in making suggestions for editing this manuscript.

About the Author

Teresa Pollard is from Richmond, Virginia, and was saved at a young age. She has a Master's degree in English and Creative Writing from Hollins College, and has served as a Sunday school teacher and children's worker for most of the last forty years. Married for forty years, she was devastated by divorce and the death of her youngest daughter, but God has blessed her with a new home and another grandson, and she now resides in Dacula, Georgia.

TeresaPollardWrites.com

facebook.com/Teresa-Pollard-327613814044009

Printed in Great Britain
by Amazon